"Quite simply, there is not a better writer of fiction now at work in the United States."
JONATHAN YARDLEY

"This collection is a widening and deepening of Taylor's already extraordinary talent for the short story."
WALKER PERCY

"Taylor's stories are beguiling, humorous, enfolding. . . . You can feel better reading them than you do when you are doing most other things; you want him to go on."
Harper's

IN
THE MIRO
DISTRICT

Peter Taylor

BALLANTINE BOOKS · NEW YORK

"In the Miro District" and "The Captain's Sons" originally appeared in *The New Yorker*. "Three Heroines" was first published in *The Virginia Quarterly Review*, "The Instruction of a Mistress" in *The New Review*, and "The Hand of Emmagene" and "Her Need" in *Shenandoah*.

Acknowledgement is made to *The Sewanee Review* for permission to reprint "The Throughway" and "Daphne's Lover." Copyright © 1964, 1969 by the University of the South.

ISBN 0-345-36405-8

This edition published by arrangement with Alfred A. Knopf, Inc.

Manufactured in the United States of America

First Ballantine Books Edition: November 1990

Contents

The Captain's Son

THERE IS AN EXCHANGE BETWEEN THE TWO
cities of Nashville and Memphis which has been going on
forever—for two centuries almost. (That's forever in Tennessee.) It's like this: A young man of good family out at
Memphis, for whom something has gone wrong, will often
take up residence in Nashville. And of course it works the
other way round. A young man in Nashville under similarly unhappy circumstances may pack up and move out
to Memphis. This continuing exchange can explain a lot
about the identical family names you find among promi-
nent people in the two places, and about the mixup and
reversal of names. Henderson Smith in one place, for instance, becomes Smith Henderson in the other. Or an ha-
bitual middle name in Nashville, say, may appear as a first
or last name in Memphis. But whether I have made this
entirely clear or not, it is an old story with us in Tennessee
and was familiar before my sister Lila and her husband,
Tolliver Bryant Campbell, were born even.

In nearly all versions of the old story the immigrant from
Memphis arrives in Nashville (or the other way round) and
falls in love at first sight with a distant connection whom
he meets by chance at a party. They get married. They
have children (giving them those mixtures of names). And
the children grow up without ever having a very clear idea

about what the original connection was or why their father chose to live in one city instead of the other.

The comical thing, though, in the case of Tolliver Campbell and my sister Lila, was that their chief connection was a quarrel—a quarrel which our two families had once had and which Tolliver, being from Memphis, still took quite seriously. For that's the way people are out at Memphis. They tend to take themselves and everything relating to themselves and their families too seriously. If Tolliver's family and ours had had a different sort of connection, he would have been no less intense about it. He was what we in Nashville used to think of as the perfect Memphis type. Yet he was not really born in Memphis. He was raised and educated out there but he was born on a cotton plantation fifty miles below Memphis—in Mississippi, which, as anybody in Nashville will tell you, is actually worse.

To my sister Lila that old family quarrel seemed merely a joke. Even Tolliver Campbell's name was not a serious-sounding name. And his own father (not his grandfather) had fought at San Juan Hill! That alone could send Lila into a fit of laughter. Our own grandfather was wartime governor of Tennessee—Spanish War (broad smiles), not Civil—and he had got Tolliver's father his captaincy! Later they quarreled, the Governor and the Captain of San Juan Hill (laughter). At our house we tended to laugh at anything that was far in the past or far in the future. We were more or less taught to. And our mother and father would say they were glad neither of us children was a young person who took himself too seriously or set too great store by who his forebears had been. We knew who we were without talking about it or thinking about it even. Simply to be what we were in Nashville, circa 1935, seemed good enough.

Well, the long-ago Captain came back from Cuba a hero. But he didn't show his face in Nashville. And he didn't come to the Wartime Governor's support when the Governor made his subsequent race for the Senate. Such an ingrate! And what a silly old business! Even Mother would throw back her head and go into gales of laughter, though it had been her papa who was governor and who *didn't* get elected to the Senate. It was all so long ago that any reference to it could set us guffawing. It was like someone's mentioning "Remember the Maine" or "Break the News to Mother."

And so when Lila came home from a dinner party and told us she had met Tolliver Campbell, who had just moved in to Nashville (it was not clear why; and Lila would have been the last person to ask), we burst into laughter— Mother and Father and I. The two of them had been seated by each other at the dinner party just by chance. Or possibly some knowing old Nashvillian had arranged the place cards that way in jest. Anyhow, what a handsome pair they made, Tolliver Bryant Campbell in his white sharkskin suit, with his dark hair and eyes, his military bearing, and his politely grave manner, there beside my pretty, vivacious, honey-haired sister Lila. Lila was twenty-one then and was reckoned a kind of second-year girl, though, since it was during the Depression, she hadn't actually come out at all. And she looked like a girl of seventeen. Tolliver himself wasn't yet thirty and so couldn't properly be termed an old bachelor. Their ages were just right for a match. They made a striking pair. When they were introduced each of them knew at once who the other was or who—within reason, considering their names—the other must be.

Lila made their meeting sound very funny, especially Tolliver's formality, especially his notion that he ought to call on Father before trying to make a real date with Lila, that he ought ("in view of past events") to explain to Father his family's version of the old quarrel, which *was* that by the time the Senate race came up Captain Campbell had married the daughter of the biggest landowner in Mississippi, a man who disapproved of his son-in-law's taking part in politics. It was a question of loyalties, don't you see? In the end, what else could the Captain do but abide by his father-in-law's wishes? Lila repeated this argument to us, but even after she and Tolliver got married my parents would never permit Tolliver to defend his father to them. At the time of the wedding, they received old Captain Campbell and Mrs. Campbell as though nothing had ever happened. The ancient quarrel was water over the dam, Mother and Father insisted, and was best forgotten. Besides, it was all too absurd. Mother was fond of saying, "It's just too absurd to be ridiculous."

On the night of the party where Tolliver and Lila met, we sat up rather later than usual at our house, the four of us in the upstairs sitting room, listening to Lila's account of her evening. In her stocking feet, but still wearing her evening dress and clutching her high-heeled slippers in one hand and her silver evening bag in the other, she went on and on about Tolliver. Then finally she announced to us—rather belatedly, we three thought—that Tolliver Campbell was, in fact, coming to pay a call on Father. What she said came as a considerable surprise—that is, after all her merriment about their meeting. Father directed a knowing grin at Mother and me and he accused Lila of having given "young Campbell" encouragement. Mother said, "Tell us the truth, Lila. You must have found the young man somewhat attractive."

Lila rolled her eyes about the room for a moment. It was as though she were summoning Tolliver's face to her mind's eye. "Oh, he's good enough looking, I guess," she said. "Like all the Campbells are. And he's rich as Croesus, everyone says." Resting her head on the chair back, she added, "But I think he's a little too Mississippi for our tastes. . . . Don't you?"

IT WAS BARELY SIX MONTHS LATER, though, that my sister Lila and Tolliver Bryant Campbell got married at the West End Methodist Church. They had a honeymoon in the Caribbean and then, at the insistence of my parents, they came to live with us at our house on Elliston Place. That they should move into the house with us was something nobody would have predicted when they first got engaged—least of all Tolliver, so it seemed. He certainly appeared to have had other plans. He had already bought a house out in the Belle Meade section, and when the decision was made about where they would live he sold the house at a shocking loss—sold it without asking my father's advice, without even trying to get a good price for the place.

They were supposed to stay with us only temporarily but they remained for more than three years. Lila would often say, with a laugh, that she and Tolliver seemed to have been struck by a paralysis of some kind. But it was Father, actually, who never quite let them go. He would always come up with a reason for them to linger another month—or another year. In the beginning I think he was afraid Tolliver might turn out to be a high liver and big spender and so, during times when nearly everybody else was hard up, be a source of embarrassment to us all.

Yet once Lila and Tolliver had settled into the house with us, what worried Father, and worried us all, was the simple fact that Tolliver Campbell had no occupation—no calling or profession of any kind. He was content to stay home every day and attend to his financial affairs—his rents and royalties, as he referred to them—sitting either at the desk in the library or at a card table in the sun parlor. He employed a secretary to come to the house twice a week, to take dictation and to attend to the most tedious details of his banking and to the bookkeeping which he had to do in connection with his landholdings. As Father pointed out, all of this was hardest on Mother. She "just wasn't prepared" to have a man around the house all the time. That might be how you did things on a Mississippi plantation, but not in Nashville. In Nashville, any man was expected to have a career of some kind. Or at least to go to an office somewhere every weekday that dawned.

I was four years younger than my sister and was just finishing high school when she married. I attended Hume-Fogg High School, the public school, because during those Depression years our family was doing whatever it decently could to cut corners. Naturally, at that time I knew precious little about any life at all outside Hume-Fogg or outside the neighborhood around Elliston Place. To have someone as different as Tolliver Campbell suddenly moving into our house, a young man so rich that he hadn't given thought to taking up some line of work—to have him living there under our roof seemed to me an extraordinary thing. He was so different from us in so many ways that we knew from the start we would have to do a lot just to make him feel comfortable with us. My mother said, in advance, that it would be only good manners to put ourselves out for him a great deal and make many allowances for him because of all that he was accustomed to having done for him at his parents' house in Memphis. She was right, of course. But as it turned out we also had to do a good many things and take a certain care just to preserve our *own* comfort, with Tolliver around. He had a way of taking you up on things you didn't quite mean for him to—such as polite offers to fetch something for him that he could very well fetch for himself. If you came into a room drinking a Coca-Cola and said politely, "Could I get you a Coke, Tolliver?" he was apt to reply, "Yes, if you would be so kind." And so you would find yourself going back to the kitchen and opening a bottle for him. Even in quite serious matters, you had to watch out for yourself.

The first time this became apparent to me was one night when Father was talking at the dinner table, over coffee. He was remarking on the high cost of everything and how the Depression had made it necessary for *everyone* to watch expenses. Tolliver was present. Though this was well before the wedding, it was after the engagement was announced and he was already coming to the house regularly. Father's remarks about economy included questions about the house Tolliver had bought and about the costs involved in its renovation. Tolliver held nothing back. For instance, he told Father exactly what the house painter's estimate "amounted to." And Father, after first carefully setting his coffee cup in its saucer, exploded in a fit of ironic laughter. "What it amounts to," he said, "is highway robbery!" And he said, still laughing, that rather than pay such bills Tolliver and Lila ought just to come and live in the house with us. How that did make us all laugh! But Tolliver's unexpected reply made us laugh even harder. "I'd just like to take you up on that, sir," he said. We thought surely he was clowning—or I did. I hadn't learned yet that Tolliver didn't ever clown.

I can see in retrospect, of course, that there was more involved that night than just Tolliver Campbell's characteristic directness. Father's own characteristic way of proceeding was involved. The fact is, he had been giving Tolliver rope. One of Father's favorite sayings was "Give a fool enough rope and he'll hang himself." He didn't consider Tolliver a fool exactly, but still he had been operating on that principle with him. He had agreed to the kind of wedding Tolliver insisted upon having. I believe he would have agreed even to their marrying at Christ Church Episcopal if Tolliver had insisted upon it, instead of at West End, which was our church. And Father had not openly protested the extravagant kind of honeymoon Tolliver and Lila were going on. When Tolliver wasn't present, of course, he had made his joke about wishing they wouldn't go so near to Cuba and maybe stir Tolliver's family memories. But he had said nothing like that to Tolliver. In retrospect it is perfectly clear to me that my father was fully prepared for that "unexpected" reply he got about their coming to live with us. As soon as we had all stopped our laughing, he said, "Well, I don't know what could suit us better, Tolliver."

As I sat there stunned by this exchange, I found it somehow reassuring to observe the smile of genuine pleasure on Father's face. Presently he glanced at Mother and me as if for support. I smiled and nodded, because I knew that's what was expected of me. Mother said, "Don't you think that before making such a momentous commitment perhaps Tolliver ought to confer privately with his bride-to-be?" But even while she was pretending to protest Mother wore a look made of all sweet accord.

Without a moment's hesitation Tolliver answered, "I've already done that, ma'am."

And as for Lila, she seemed even more delighted than Father by the prospect. "It's a grand idea," she said, "if Tolliver thinks he can stand having so many of us around him for a while." It was evident how thoroughly she and Tolliver had already gone into the subject.

Mother said, "We'll certainly try to make you comfortable here, Tolliver."

It seemed a victory for Tolliver at the time. It appeared he was still having his way, as he had been allowed to have it about the wedding plans (a large church wedding with all of Nashville and half of Memphis invited, with eight bridesmaids and groomsmen, and a reception at the Centennial Club afterward; Father said that when the Campbell clan came down the aisle he was himself going to step forward and sing "The Campbells are coming, I owe, I owe!") and as he had been allowed to have it about where they would go on their honeymoon. (Mother thought it would seem less ostentatious, in view of how hard the times were for most people, if they merely went for a week's stay at Flat Rock. But Tolliver insisted upon his romantic notion that it wouldn't seem like a real honeymoon if they didn't cross over a border somewhere.) But it only *seemed* that Tolliver was once again having his own way. Looking back, I cannot imagine he and Lila would have been permitted to set up a house of their own, especially not in a house of the grand sort that Tolliver had bought in Belle Meade. If they had been allowed to, one can't know what might have happened or how happily it all might have turned out. They might be living right here in Nashville and might have a house full of children with a scramble of names from our two families.

But I think even Tolliver may have shared Father's uneasy feeling that the Campbell affluence might become a source of embarrassment to us. Tolliver Campbell seemed to want to have some sort of restraint put upon himself. I don't know how else to explain his behavior. I have never since seen a young man who so plainly felt the urgency to marry not just a certain girl but that girl's whole family. And I suppose it was merely a fatal coincidence that my parents felt a similar compulsion to take Tolliver Campbell completely under their wing—even if it meant having him there in the house.

The worst of it was, he was always there. He found our house infinitely comfortable. And clearly our way of living in it was just as much to his liking. There were the afternoons when he played tennis and the afternoons when he played bridge and the evening hours when he and Lila were usually out with their friends. But, except for those times, one was apt to come upon him at any hour almost anywhere in the house. I had never before fully realized what great opportunities for comfort our house afforded or how many cozy corners we had. It got so I could wander into a room and sit down without observing for some time that he was present. It was as if Tolliver Campbell had become more at home in our house than we were ourselves. When suddenly I did see him, he simply gazed over his newspaper or his book or his pipe or raised his eyes from his game of solitaire and smiled at me warmly. And then he went on with whatever he was doing. His smile seemed to say, "Isn't this great, our life in this house?" Sometimes Lila would be there beside him and they would be playing double sol or reading from the same newspaper or just talking so quietly that you could not really hear them across the room. But Lila would still smile at you in her old way as if she were suppressing a giggle about the situation. This was surprising to me, because I somehow felt that it meant she wasn't taking her marriage seriously. But often as not I wouldn't really notice whether Lila was with him. I would just register his presence and his smile and think how extraordinary it was for a grown man to be at home so much and to behave so like somebody my age, like a teen-ager lounging around the house in the summertime.

Yet you couldn't help liking *his* liking his life with us so much. It inevitably made you speculate on how he must have hated his life in Memphis. If he had had more frankness in his nature, if he had been a more talkative person than he was, he would surely—or so I used to imagine—have said how much he preferred my parents to his own parents out at Memphis and preferred our kind of household to theirs.

The truth is, we knew quite well by this time that Tolliver's parents were the "something" in Memphis that had gone wrong in his life. Once he and Lila were safely married, once they had been pronounced man and wife, and when we were all finally leaving the Centennial Club reception and were about to take the bride and groom to their train, Tolliver called Father aside to thank him for everything and to tell him also—at what he considered the first appropriate moment—his reason for having left Memphis and come to Nashville to live. I don't know how long before that night Father had already known all about it, but I am sure he *had* known. Perhaps he knew the night when, over coffee, he committed Tolliver to coming to live with us. Perhaps Tolliver knew he knew even then. Perhaps everyone except me knew, and that only because I was thought too young to know. But even I knew from the first moment that the senior Campbells arrived in Nashville for the wedding. They stepped down from their Pullman car, early on the morning of the wedding, both of them reeking so of alcohol that I saw the colored porter who had received their tip turn away with a pained expression.

At the wedding itself they both clearly were so drunk that each had to be supported as they walked down the aisle on the arm of an usher. It was at the reception that I got my best look at them. I was at an age when I knew almost nothing about such matters, of course, but I did have the distinct impression that they were the best-dressed people present; that, despite a certain disarray in their clothes, they were of the highest style. And I was aware of how well nature had endowed them both, of what good-looking people they were, or had once been. And though they were among the oldest people present, it was hard for me to think of them as such. What was most difficult of all was to remember that he was none other than Captain Lester Campbell of the Spanish-American War and San Juan Hill.

There was only a fruit punch served at the reception, but the senior Campbells staggered about, unable to make any sensible conversation, now and then disappearing into the rest rooms and reappearing noticeably refreshed but wearing a stunned expression on their faces, as though they were not quite sure where they were or what company they were in. Finally they were taken away to their train to Memphis by a person obviously in the employ of Tolliver and described by him as a "hired chauffeur." It was then that Tolliver asked Father if he might have a few words with him in private. Looking Father directly in the eye, and with no apology in his manner, he told him that from his earliest recollection both his parents had been in and out of the famous Memphis sanitarium that treated alcoholics in those days, committed sometimes the one by the other, sometimes both of them by Tolliver himself after he came of age. He told Father that they were well known in Memphis (as Father no doubt already knew) for their public fights with each other and their brawling at the Country Club or at the Silver Slipper or on the Peabody Hotel Roof. Tolliver had finally bolted and come to Nashville, but only after years of degrading experiences at home and endless humiliation in public and only after he had realized at last that he could no longer be of help to them and could not make a satisfactory life of his own while continuing to live in the same city with them.

Father tried to reassure him. He said how sad it was that a person with Tolliver's fine qualities should have been born into such a situation and brought up in such a world. "Yes," said Tolliver, manifesting an impatient satisfaction, "yes." But the "yes" did not imply that he agreed with Father. It seemed to mean that this was just the line he had known Father would take. And that the real purpose of their exchange was for him to dispel any notion on Father's part that he was not happy and proud to be who and what he was. It was not till a number of years later that Father reported the incident to me. It was his impression then that Tolliver had taken this opportunity—that it had perhaps

12

been the sole purpose of his ostensible revelation—to say that although he rejected his parents' alcoholism he did not reject the kind of Deep South Planter life that he and his kind were heir to, and did not accept the idea that a life of leisure, supported by the labor of others or maintained by an unearned income, was necessarily an immoral sort of existence. "I regret that my parents have been destroyed by their weakness for bourbon whiskey," he said. "But that doesn't mean I discount my good luck in having been born their son or having grown up in their house. I look forward to living in your house for a time, sir," he concluded, "but, still, remember that I come there as my father's son." Then he added that he had waited till after the wedding ceremony to speak of his parents' unhappy state because otherwise he would have been speaking of it to someone outside his family. That was all he said. After that night he never made reference to the subject again. And we never again set eyes on Captain and Mrs. Campbell.

I MUST SAY SOMETHING NOW ABOUT THE drinking habits—or, more precisely, the non-drinking habits—of my own parents during those years. From the day that the Eighteenth Amendment became law no liquor was served in our house. My father even gave up his toddy before dinner. The only liquor in the house was kept under lock and key in a cabinet in his bedroom. And then, fourteen years later, on the day when the Repeal became official, Father brought forth his bottle of bourbon and renewed his old habit of a single toddy before dinner and a neat jigger at bedtime. This observance of the law of the land was not so strait-laced or unusual on his part as it may sound. Other people like my parents, in Nashville, were as strict about observing the changeable laws of the land as they were about observing their own unchangeable codes of decent conduct. We had a cousin, a federal judge, who declined to serve alcoholic drinks throughout the period of national Prohibition. His younger friends assumed that he had never during his life served drinks and that it was out of personal conviction. They always fortified themselves well before going to dinner at the Judge's house. At his first party after the Repeal, the guests came as usual in a fortified state. When the Judge served cocktails that night, the young people all got shockingly drunk. Deciding Prohibition had been a good thing after all, the Judge never again served liquor.

My father, even in those days, even in a Southern place like Nashville, thought that, since it was the law of the land, Negro people ought to be allowed to vote. He would sometimes make special trips home from town to take our servants to register and to vote, just to make sure there was no interference with what was supposed to be. Only our old cook Betsy refused to go along with him. "Don't come bothering me about voting," said she. "That's something white folks know how to do, and what I say is, Let the white folks do any little old thing for themselves that they can do."

But my parents were not merely law-abiding. And they did not merely conform to social conventions. They believed that they acted always from the right instincts—right instincts which they shared with all the sensible and well-bred people they knew in Nashville. During the Depression they entertained very little, because they thought it would look bad to be dressing up and giving parties, as if to show that they had been sensible enough to stash something away when there were so many people of their own background who had not. To have done otherwise would have revealed a lack of the right instinct. And it was for the same reason, really, that Lila had been discouraged from making her début. Similar reasoning no doubt had something to do with their wish to bring Tolliver Campbell to live in our house. Wasn't *everybody's* son-in-law coming to live with them in those difficult days? And if your son-in-law were very rich and saw fit to come and live with you, weren't you and he the most sensible, most modest people of all?

AS I HAVE INDICATED, TOLLIVER NEVER EX-pressly praised our way of living. No more than he ever made direct references to the shortcomings of his parents or to what his parents had provided him or failed to provide him in the way of an upbringing. But sometimes when I came in from school he would look on as Mother and Lila and I seated ourselves around the dining-room table and reported to each other the events of our day. Usually old Betsy would come through the pantry and, standing with the swinging door half open, would ask me what I had done-eat for lunch. If I had had the very kind of cake she had baked that day, she would say, "Oh, pshaw!" But she would always manage to produce some other sweet that I liked, and bring it and a glass of milk and set them before me on the bare table.

"You are a lucky young fellow," Tolliver would say then. That was the nearest he came to saying anything direct about his upbringing. But once, when I was in the hammock out in the yard and somebody called to ask if I wanted a slice of cake or a piece of pie, he told me about some friend or other of his in Memphis, somebody that he, when he was my age, used to go home with sometimes after school, and how his friend's family seemed always to be just sitting around, laughing and talking with each other, telling each other everything there was to tell about themselves, and making no pretense about anything whatsoever, and expressing no dissatisfaction with the life they had.

When I reported to my father how Tolliver implied a comparison between us and those people in Memphis, Father sat smiling to himself. Then he broke into derisive laughter. Of *course* Tolliver knew people like us in Memphis! And was kin to them, too. Anyone would know that. And didn't Tolliver think we had just such relatives as the Campbells? Of *course* we did have. Even I didn't need to be told that. We had many rich cousins in New York and St. Louis and Chicago. And we had any number of them right in Nashville, for that matter! But from Father's tone of voice I knew the kind of relative that he was talking about: We had what he called our Old South cousins. Some of them lived around Nashville, out on the various pikes and lanes toward Brentwood. They kept horses and rode to hounds and lived in antebellum houses or in houses built to look antebellum. But most of our cousins and connections of that sort lived a little farther off, in such snooty old towns as Franklin and Gallatin and Shelbyville. They would talk to you as though Gallatin or Franklin, for instance, were places as big as Nashville or Memphis. It was as though they were all of them blind and couldn't see what a city Nashville had become and didn't know what a difference that made in the way you looked at things. They thought too much of themselves and their pasts to observe that some places and some people in Tennessee had changed and had kept up with the times. Moreover, Father always reminded us, too, that we had country kin who were poor as church mice and would never be anything but dirt farmers. He said he didn't like one sort any better than he did the other. He said he thought everybody ought to manage to be merely representative, and ought to be modest about who they were and what they had. "The Campbells have plenty of poor, up-country kin, too," he said. "But the Campbells are people who have always managed to marry *up*—in one sense or another. I hope that may never be said of us."

WHEN TOLLIVER AND LILA HAD BEEN MAR-ried about two years my parents suddenly began to entertain. At first Lila made humorous references to this entertaining, though without being really critical of it. She said, "Don't you see you're upsetting Tolliver's routine?" She meant there was always a flurry of housecleaning on the day people were coming to dinner and that Tolliver had to keep shifting from room to room to get out of old Betsy's way. But, more important, she meant that Tolliver had to dress for dinner, had to put on his tuxedo and participate in the party. Because it was soon apparent, even to me, that it was for Tolliver that the parties were given. The dinner guests were for the most part (as Mother would have said, and no doubt did say to Father in private) sensible, representative people like themselves—representative, one supposes, of the old social values in Nashville, people who maintained standards that only they could understand and that even their children never pretended to understand entirely, people who did nothing to excess, especially who did not fail or succeed in life to excess. But sprinkled among these, from the first, would be a cousin or two, from Gallatin or Shelbyville, say, who had great tone. And then, always, there would be an example of what Father would previously have spoken of laughingly as Nashville's business tycoons, a shoe manufacturer or an insurance executive, who was happy—or whose wife was happy—to meet those horsy, high-living, Middle Tennessee, non-Nashville relatives of ours. Those dinner parties were actually rather swell affairs, with Mother producing from her store of possessions silver and plate and crystal and table linen that Lila and I hardly knew existed. Even at the time of the wedding there had been no such display. At each party, one of the out-of-town Old South kin would be the guest of honor— guests of honor, I should say, because they always came in couples, of course—and naturally it was they who would be seated at Mother's and Father's right. And however else the seating might be arranged, Tolliver would invariably be seated directly across from the business tycoon. And inevitably Tolliver would, a few days afterward, receive an invitation to lunch with the man. It became as clear as Mother's best crystal that Father was determined now to find Tolliver a career, an occupation which would finally get him out of the house during daylight hours.

The offers of jobs that came to Tolliver—even offers of partnerships, offers to let him buy into something good— were discussed openly in the family. During this period Father emerged from a state of gloom that had been of many months' duration, a state of which I, and possibly the rest of the family, had not taken sufficient notice. To resort to those entertainments that he and Mother gave, for him to actually initiate such a program, undoubtedly constituted an act of desperation. But he and Mother had obviously realized that there *had* to be a change. Tolliver's comfort in our house had become my father's utter discomfort. Although I frequently failed to observe Tolliver's presence in a room, Father could step inside the front door and sense in precisely what spot in the house his son-in-law was "lolling." "Lolling" was of course not the correct word, though it was the word Father used. Tolliver never lolled in his life. He always sat fairly erect in a chair, and his attention was always occupied by a game or by some matter of his income or by his thorough perusal of the daily newspaper and the various weekly magazines that came to us. Father never failed to ask him what he was reading— especially if, as sometimes, he had a book instead of the newspaper or a magazine in his hand—and then Father's only comment would be a snort of laughter. Tolliver always rose when Father addressed him. He gave Father the title of the book or the subject of the article, but he never said more than that. Father's snort of laughter was Tolliver's signal to sit down again and return to his reading. And after pretending to suppress further signs of amusement Father would go off into another room and close the door.

The discussions of Tolliver's job offers were not discussions of how worthwhile they might be for him but of the nature of each particular line of business or segment of industry. Tolliver would reveal that he had considerable information on the subject at hand and could reel off impressive statistics. He was willing to discuss with us types of business organization, methods of production, distribution, et cetera. But he always ended it there, making it clear that he understood what it was that was being offered him, but also that it was something that he could not by any stretch of the imagination interest himself in.

At last it was the Governor of Tennessee himself that my parents had to dinner. The Governor's wife was my mother's second cousin—not that that had anything to do with their being invited or with their acceptance of the invitation, either. Before the Depression, we had always made a practice of having each new governor and his lady to dinner. My father was not directly influential in politics, but it goes without saying, I suppose, that we were the kind of people whose invitation to dinner a governor recently arrived in Nashville was not likely to refuse. The long and the short of it was, Tolliver was asked up to the Capitol the very next week and was offered a place on the Governor's staff. When the subject of his offer came up at home, over coffee that night—it was Mother's rule that subjects which might possibly be controversial should not be introduced until the meal was substantially over—Tolliver tried to dismiss it with a shake of his head and with the application of a new match to his pipe. There was no discussion of the job itself or of how the state government functioned. That, of course, would have been superfluous in our company. Father gazed up at the ceiling for a long time. The room was silent except for Tolliver's raspy drawing on his pipe. Finally Father dropped his eyes to his hands, which he had clasped before him. Then he looked up at Tolliver, a self-deprecating smile on his face, and said, "As your father-in-law I ask you to accept the Governor's appointment."

The silence in the room seemed to deepen. Tolliver didn't even take another draw on his pipe. Mother's suggestion that we all "go into the other room" to finish our coffee was very welcome. And two days later Tolliver reported to the Governor's office on the main floor of the Capitol building.

BY THIS TIME I WAS IN MY SECOND YEAR OUT at the University—at Vanderbilt, that is—but I still lived at home because of the money it saved us. And though I spent a lot of time at my fraternity house I always came home for dinner at night and frequently I came in during the early afternoon. I remember two or three times having the feeling that something was missing in the house. It was Tolliver, of course. He wasn't over there in the leather chair in the library, with his book or his newspaper, and wasn't on the wicker settee in the sun parlor, with a game of old sol going on the cushion beside him. This happened only two or three times, though. Because it was just a matter of weeks after he went to work for the Governor that I came home one afternoon and found him again in the upstairs sitting room. It was just as it had been before. I didn't notice he was in the room at first. I wandered into the room, eating a bowl of dry cereal with sugar and cream and a sliced banana on it. My thoughts must have been on something over at the University. When I saw him I was so startled that I almost dropped the china cereal bowl. I was startled beyond all reason, much more than I had been even the first time I ever came into a room without realizing he was present. It seems to me now at least that I sensed at once that his being over there would never be *quite* the same as his being there before had been. I asked him if he had "a holiday or something." He said no, he was home to stay. He just wasn't cut out, he said, for the kind of work required of somebody on a governor's staff. He said not an hour of the day passed without your having to tell a big lie or do something else that went against the grain. "You know what I mean, don't you, Brother?" he said. ("Brother" was what Lila and my parents always called me. This was the first time Tolliver had taken it up, and I was never to hear him use it again.) I said I did understand, of course—though I didn't at all know what he meant. After a second he said, "I thought *you* might." Clearly he saw now that I didn't. And I felt terribly guilty. I felt that, if I had let him, he would have talked to me about things long before this. And that he would never try again. I felt vaguely responsible somehow for whatever was going to happen now, though I could not have said why. I got out of the room as fast as I could. When I went back downstairs I found Mother and Lila in the front part of the house, in the living room. They had been talking and they went on talking. I ambled into the big front room and sat down, still taking a spoonful of cereal now and then. They saw me, naturally, yet they seemed really unaware that I had sat down there in the room with them.

They had already been over Tolliver's resignation a number of times. They had covered that ground and now they were preparing themselves for Father's coming home from town. They would tell him all about it at once, they agreed. There was no use postponing it. "The inevitable result must be—" said Mother, standing before Lila, who was seated on the couch. "The end result will be—though it will not be to my liking, Lila—that you and Tolliver must find a house of your own now. You must console yourself with that. No matter what bitter words Father may utter and how difficult the moment may be, you must bear in mind that it all means that you will finally have a place of your own. I am sure that is something you must have wished for many times, dear."

Lila, in her characteristic way, dropped her head on the back of the couch and let her eyes roll about the room. "Well, no," she said at last. "It can't be that, Mother. That *can't* be the outcome."

"I am afraid, in the end, it will have to be that," Mother insisted.

"No it *can't* be that, Mother," Lila repeated, with new firmness in her tone. "Not yet."

I could tell from Mother's expression, and Lila obviously could tell too, that Mother thought that something had happened to Tolliver Campbell's fortune, that his money was gone.

Lila gave way to giggles. Then, pulling herself up, she said, "It's worse than you think, Mother darling. We can't, we *must not* go to a house of our own. I couldn't quite face that now. It's too late. Or maybe it's only too soon. You see, Tolliver and I are not really married."

"Lila, do be serious for once in your life."

"I have never been more serious, Mother. You might as well know now that what we call our marriage is a marriage that has never been consummated."

Mother was plainly unable to speak for half a minute or so. Lila sat looking at her. Finally Lila said, "You mustn't ask me what it is he and I have been waiting on—or what *he* has been waiting on—for I can't tell you." Then the two of them looked at each other for a longer time without speaking.

At last Mother sat down on the fire bench and said, "Lila, my dear unhappy child, why haven't you spoken before? But it is not too late. Don't you see this may be a godsend? It may be that it's the privacy of his own house he has been waiting on?"

"Except that he didn't ever really want a house," Lila said. "That house he bought was just to make him seem serious about things. And he didn't really want a wife. He's a little boy still. He never *was* what he seemed. He wasn't the mysterious young man I imagined him to be, whose immoral life had made his leaving Memphis a necessity. He's only a little boy. What he wanted of us here was a mama and a papa and a little sister and maybe a little brother." Suddenly she looked over at me and snickered.

Now Mother was saying, "That may be how it *was*, Lila, and how it *has* been. But it is up to you from this moment forward, daughter. You must change matters. You know what I mean, don't you?"

"Yes," said Lila, "even Brother over there knows what you mean, Mother." My mother looked at me and blushed. She had completely forgotten my presence. Perhaps it would be true to say that for the moment she had forgotten my existence even. I think it must have been among the worst moments in her life. I rose to leave, and Lila said— more to me than to Mother, it seemed—"It's not up to me. It never will be up to me. It's still up to Tolliver. It's his problem, and he must solve it in his own way, whatever that may turn out to be." I could hear Mother crying now as I went out through the dining room toward the pantry.

MY MOTHER NEVER KEPT ANYTHING FROM my father. And so there was no doubt that before the next morning he knew all that she knew about the state of affairs. At dinner nothing was said of Tolliver's failure at the State House and nothing, of course, of his failure upstairs. After dinner Tolliver and Lila went out for a while, and I noticed that Tolliver had his briefcase with him. But they didn't dress up as they usually did when they were going out for the evening. And they were back within less than an hour, with Tolliver still lugging his briefcase. They went directly up to their room and they did not reappear until lunchtime the following day. It was something that had never happened before. But during the two following spring months it was never any other way than that. They would disappear upstairs immediately after dinner at night, and we wouldn't see them again until noon the next day. Our house was one of those big houses built in Nashville around the turn of the century, and the walls were fairly soundproof. But sometimes in the night, during this period, I would hear Lila's and Tolliver's voices coming from their room. Sometimes they would seem to be laughing almost hysterically, and sometimes I was sure both voices were raised in anger. And no one was allowed in their room at any time during those months. Even old Betsy wasn't let in to change the linen. On a few occasions, at the beginning, they went out with some of their friends to dinner. And I would hear Lila locking the bedroom door as they left. Soon they altogether gave up seeing their friends in the evening. Lila seldom left the house. Often she returned to their room after lunch. Tolliver had now begun leaving the house to play either bridge or tennis every afternoon—even on the weekend. During all this, my parents struck me as being in a kind of daze. Most of the time they didn't even make conversation with each other.

Then one morning early in June, Tolliver appeared at the breakfast table, though without sitting down to join us. He announced that he had rented a small office a few blocks away from the house. He planned to go there every morning and attend to all of his business matters. Father looked up at him and smiled uncertainly. It seemed to me it was the first time he had smiled at all for two months past. I thought I read hope in the smile as it began to spread across his face. Then as the smile became more fully formed and expressive I saw that what it clearly expressed was regret. I understood Father's feeling at once: Why couldn't Tolliver have made such a gesture six months earlier? It would have mattered then. It didn't matter now to any of us. It was too late—though I could sense that even Father didn't know exactly why it was too late. He and Mother were sitting across the table from me. Tolliver was standing at the place just beside me. It was apparent he was not going to have breakfast with us. He just stood there behind the chair, with his two hands on the chair back. I could barely keep from fixing my eyes on his gold wedding band, but I managed to look up at his face, and I heard Mother saying, "You will be better able to concentrate on your work in an office, won't you?" As she spoke, and as I watched Tolliver's face, I thought that in his brown eyes there was none of the respect and admiration for my parents that formerly one always read there. Afterward, it seemed to me I had read in his eyes that morning a certain vengeful gleam. But I can never be certain of that. At any rate, while I looked at him I became aware of something considerably more powerful than anything that his eyes expressed. He smelled the way some of the older boys in my fraternity did on the morning after a big drunk. And I had smelled it once before, on the platform at the Union Depot. It was the odor, at once sour and musky, of a person whose system has been saturated with bourbon whiskey. I could imagine almost that he was standing close to me on purpose, so that I would be sure to smell him. Once I had recognized the odor, the vaguely bloodshot eyes and the tired expression about the mouth were unmistakable signs. He was like a hung-over fraternity boy with an eight-o'clock class to make.

I said nothing until he had gone. But when he had lumbered out through the front hall with his briefcase and pulled the front door behind him, I said at once, "Boy! Has *he* been boozing!"

Almost before the words were out of my mouth Father said, "Nonsense! What idiocy has come over you? You don't know what you are talking about."

And Mother said, "I often wonder, Brother, what it is you *are* learning over at Vanderbilt University!"

With my two parents' eyes on me I began eating my breakfast again. Though I could recognize the outrage in their faces and knew that nothing I might add would convince them if they did not already believe me, I did say, with my mouth full of food, "I'm just telling you. He's been boozing. And I don't mean he's just had a 'social' drink or two." I felt as though this were almost the first observation about a member of my family that I had ever made for myself, and I knew I had to insist upon it.

"Well," Father said, "*I'm* telling you to keep such mistaken observations to yourself."

Still I did not give in. He got up from the table and kissed Mother goodbye. But before he had got halfway across the front hall, there was a noise from upstairs, a loud thump, as though a piece of furniture had fallen over or someone had dropped a heavy object. Father turned and moved quickly toward the foot of the stairs. Mother sprang up from the table and overtook him. "Let me go to her, dear," she said.

At the top of the stairway she knocked on Lila's door. And she called her name. "May I come in, Lila?" she asked.

Lila's voice rang out: "No, you may not. You may not come in here. It's *my* room, and Tolliver's!"

"What's happened, darling?"

"You just may not come in. Do you hear me? You just may *not*."

Mother glanced down the steps at Father. He nodded.

"Go in," he whispered. Mother tried the door to see if it was locked. It wasn't. She cracked the door, leaning forward. She seemed frozen in that position for several seconds. Presently she made a gesture, indicating that Father and I should stay downstairs. I think Father would have gone on up except that he knew I would follow, sheeplike, and he was afraid there was something up there that I shouldn't see.

He and I might as well have gone up, because when Mother came down, half an hour later, she concealed nothing, not even from me. She described what she had seen so graphically that I have ever afterward imagined that I actually did look into the room with her. As she opened the door she beheld Lila stark naked except for her hat and shoes and just picking herself up—herself and her handbag—from where she had fallen, in the center of the large room. She had plainly been preparing to come downstairs and then go out on the streets of Nashville just as she was. She seemed unaware that the only clothing she had put on was her narrow-brimmed straw hat and her spectator pumps. Mother said to us, "In the old days, before Prohibition, I saw any number of drunk persons in all kinds of public places in Nashville. But Lila is the most thoroughly inebriated person I have ever set eyes on." Upstairs she had struggled with Lila to get her into her nightgown and then back into bed. She was able to do so, she told us, only after making a solemn promise to Lila. "And," she asserted, more to herself now than to us, "I intend to keep my promise to her."

While she seemed to be wandering off in her own reflections, Father declared, "The first thing is to get a doctor here." That recalled Mother from her reverie.

"No," she asserted, "there will be no doctor here. Our concern from here out is to protect Lila. And only that. She is married to an unholy fiend. Since he is her lawful husband, we may not be able to protect her from him, but we can protect her from the eyes of the world. Within a few months he has managed to reduce her to a complete dependence upon liquor. He has done it right here in our house. You should see the room. The mantel shelf and the tops of the bureaus are lined with empty bottles."

I could not make out from what she said whether she thought Tolliver, as he had turned to drinking himself, had done this thing unconsciously or had purposely corrupted Lila. The question would occupy my mind for a long time and of course no one—possibly not even Tolliver—could ever give an assured answer to it. And now Mother was saying to Father, "I want you to go to your liquor cabinet and bring me a bottle of bourbon whiskey. That's what she's come to like. If I give her one drink now, she says she will sleep till noon. That's become her practice."

During the hours before lunchtime I wondered if Tolliver would come back for lunch or even if he would ever come back at all. I doubted that the office he spoke of existed. It seemed possible that, with full knowledge of her present condition and probably what was her fixed habit, he had left her in the house without any liquor and without the means of obtaining any unless she came downstairs to beg some of her father or went out in the town somewhere to purchase it. In either case she was bound to expose her wretched condition to her parents. On the other hand, in his own present hung-over state it seemed possible—even quite likely—that Tolliver was incapable of such purposeful action. The worst possibility—and one which I could not even entertain—was that Tolliver was so base as to have consciously planned an act of vengeance months before and was now mindlessly carrying it out.

WE WERE ALL SOMEWHAT REASSURED WHEN Tolliver did return for lunch. Father had been persuaded by Mother to go on downtown as usual. It is hard to believe he was able to concentrate on his work there. I was supposed to be studying for my examinations, and so I stayed at home all morning, but only pretending to study, actually waiting to see if there was any word from Tolliver. He came in at noon with the predictable briefcase, and went directly up to his and Lila's room. At half past twelve he and Lila and Mother and I sat down to lunch in the dining room. Since Father never came home to lunch, he was not there. But Mother had gone to the telephone and called him to report Tolliver's return the moment it occurred. My first thought when Tolliver opened the front door was how I dreaded the four of us sitting down at the table together. But, though I doubted my own senses almost, it was no different from other lunches in past months. And I knew then that dinner that night would be no different from other dinners. It was not like old times before Tolliver resigned his place on the Governor's staff, but it was like all the times since his resignation. There was no laughing or giggling on our part and no warm smiles on the part of Tolliver. And at dinner that night Father did not, of course, tease or attempt any of his old jokes. But still there was merely a subdued or modulated tone to our talk and to our behavior in general. The fact is, that noon and that night I observed changes which had clearly taken place but which had escaped me before or which I had been unwilling to take cognizance of. Lila was no longer my pretty second-year-girl sister, careless of what she said in the bosom of the family and making her giggly comments on everything. I felt that even the way she asked for a second cup of coffee nowadays was different. She considered how it would sound. Would she seem to be *needing* too much coffee? But what was more noticeable even was that before answering any question at all—of the least consequence—she would glance at Tolliver. I noticed, too, that the same, more or less, was true of Tolliver. Whenever a remark was addressed to him, he would glance at Lila before responding. They had become exclusively dependent upon each other—in a way that was altogether unpleasant to the rest of us. We seemed no longer a real part of their existence. It is hard for me to believe that my parents had not noticed such changes or had not detected at some time or other—even though *I* had failed to—the smell of alcohol on their breath or the odor of alcohol in the vicinity of their bedroom. But I must confess that from that day forward it became harder for me to understand the behavior of my parents than that of my alcoholic sister and brother-in-law.

The incident of that morning wasn't again mentioned within my hearing. There was never any mention made, either, of the drinking that had gone on upstairs in the past months and that continued to go on up there. Sometimes in the night one would still hear voices—drunken voices, as I thought of them now—but that of course was never commented upon. The only oblique reference, even, made to what had happened came on the Sunday afternoon following the incident.

It was just after our big midday Sunday meal. I was still studying for my exams. I drifted into the library, intending to look up something in the encyclopedia. Suddenly I became aware that Tolliver and Lila were talking quietly in a corner of the room. Mother and Father observed my quick withdrawal from the library and were able to surmise what it meant. Father began talking to me at once about how happy he and Mother had been from the very start to have Lila and Tolliver live with us. Presently Mother commenced repeating her old bit about our wanting to make Tolliver comfortable. Only this time it was Tolliver's *and* Lila's comfort she referred to. She and Father both insisted that their feelings about this had not changed at all. Mother, who only those few months before had spoken plainly to Lila about the desirability of their finding another place to live, now said that Lila and Tolliver must not be tempted by anything any of us said or did to leave our house and go into a house of their own.

"We are thinking only of their own good," Father said. "It would be a costly, a very dangerous move for them."

From then on there could be no doubt that my parents had only one concern: Tolliver and Lila must not be subjected to the public gaze of Nashville. Lila was hardly ever allowed to leave the house without Mother at her side. It was even suggested that the upstairs sitting room be converted into an office for Tolliver. Above all, life in the house must go on just as it had before, so long as Tolliver and Lila could be kept at home. The only obvious change was that Tolliver, instead of accepting the offer of the sitting room, continued to rise early every morning—though not so early as on that first day—and set out for his office, always without breakfast, always with his briefcase in hand. Meanwhile, Lila continued to sleep every morning until almost noon.

My two parents did seem to regain some of their old spirit and composure. Or at least they feigned it. Sometimes at the dinner table Father would actually make a sort of imitation of his old jokes. And Lila would make a feeble effort to respond with something like a girlish giggle. It went on like that all summer. Since I had failed two of my examinations, I went to summer school and was away from the house even more than in the winter. I even spent a good many nights at the fraternity house. It was mostly empty, and so I didn't have to pay to stay there. I did my first real drinking that summer, and from time to time all of us who were putting up there brought girls to the house, which was on Twenty-third Avenue and only a few blocks from Elliston Place. I don't know that that has any relevance except that I embraced almost any opportunity that summer that might help me interpret for myself what was going on at home.

Then, toward the end of August, at Sunday dinner, Tolliver announced that he was going to make a trip to Memphis that week—to attend to some business there. He had barely taken his seat at the table when he made the announcement. Father had just begun to carve the hen and he continued with his carving. Still not looking at Tolliver, he said, "I wasn't listening carefully just now. But did I understand you to say, Tolliver, that you were *moving* to Memphis—you and Lila?" He looked up then with a smile on his face which would allow Tolliver to take what he said as a joke if he so wished. I may have imagined it but I thought I saw a blush rising in Tolliver's cheek. He didn't speak until he had accepted a plate and passed it on to Mother. When he did speak, he enunciated with great care, as if to make certain there was no misunderstanding: "Yes, sir. The fact is, Lila and I have decided to buy a house in Memphis, and I am going out there this week to look around." Lila's face told me nothing. There was no telling whether or not she and Tolliver had really discussed such a plan before. She was in perfect control. But when I glanced at my mother I saw at once that she and Father had already gone into this possibility very thoroughly.

I went back to the fraternity house that afternoon and spent the night there. I didn't have a girl or do any drinking. I sat on the upstairs porch with my feet on the banister railing half the night, thinking about what had happened and then trying for a while, now and then, not to think about it.

WITHIN TWO WEEKS LILA AND TOLLIVER had bought a house in Memphis. Within less than a month, before the fall session began at Vanderbilt, they took their leave of Elliston Place. Only on the morning of their departure did Lila manage to get up in time for breakfast. They had done all their packing during the previous day or two. (I don't know what ever became of all the bottles. They were not in the room when I went up to help with their luggage. Perhaps they went out as they came in, two at a time in Tolliver's briefcase.) Lila drank her coffee but ate almost no breakfast. There was again no mistaking the odor of liquor about her or Tolliver. As they sat down at the table, I suddenly remembered the ugly face the porter had made when the senior Campbells got off the train on the morning of the wedding. But Father and Mother didn't bat an eye, much less turn up a nose. You would have thought we had never had a bad moment in the house and that Lila and Tolliver were off on a lark to Memphis or were facing some bright new prospect out there. We said our goodbyes at the curb, and Father said that he would have the wedding presents, which were all stored in our attic, sent on to them within a week. Mother said she could hardly wait to come out and see their house.

But she and Father never made such a trip to visit them in Memphis. Sometimes Lila would come home for a one-night stay. No more than that, though. From then on, Lila and Tolliver lived always in Memphis. They had one child, a son. He was not named for Father or for our family at all but for his Campbell grandfather, who died just before the baby was born.

Both my mother and my father are dead now and have been dead for several years. After Lila and Tolliver left Nashville—that fall—I decided to try living in the fraternity house, despite all Father had to say about the expense of it. And though I have never married, I never lived at home again. After Vanderbilt, I took an apartment in one of the suburban developments off Hillsboro Road. There was no pressure at all put on me to move back to Elliston Place.

Mother and Father continued to live there alone during the rest of their lives, dying within a few months of each other.

Nowadays, two or three times a year I get a letter from Lila. One letter will be full of her old fun or full of reminiscences about her childhood. But the next may make no sense at all. Or there will be one that is almost entirely illegible and that I don't work very hard at deciphering, because I can see at a glance it consists mostly of complaints about troubles they are having with their son. It is easy to imagine the kind of life she and Tolliver have had out there. (And what a life the boy must have had, growing up with them!) It sometimes seems a wonder to me that they have managed to stick together at all. Yet I know couples just like them right here in Nashville. Something happened to them that nobody but the very two of them could ever understand. And so they can't separate. They are too dependent on each other and on the good bourbon whiskey they drink together. Theirs is a sort of joint boozing that sustains them in a way that solitary boozing or casual boozing with a stranger or even with some old friend can't do. They go on drinking together year after year. If their livers stand up under it, they may actually survive to a very old age. In fact, one imagines sometimes, waking in the middle of the night and thinking about them, that Tolliver and Lila just might have the bad luck to live forever— the two of them, together in that expensive house they bought, perched among other houses just like it, out there on some godforsaken street in the flat and sun-baked and endlessly sprawling purlieus of Memphis.

The Instruction of a Mistress

1. An entry in his journal

I taught her everything she knows.
All she was capable of teaching me
Was how to drive a car.
And what use could that be
To me, living all winter on Central Park West
And all summer at the Vineyard?
Her teaching me to drive
That week in the Poconos
Was merely an exercise in patience
On my part. What I was actually learning
On that honeymoon, if you please, of ours
Was just how much there was
How many realms there were
That I would have to be her teacher in.

Well, I taught her more in five years
Than she might otherwise have learnt in twenty—
About art and literature and even foreign languages.
So what's all this fuss about now?
Only let it be said: I was her college education.
We were together those five long years
And now, by God, it's done. And those things I've men-
tioned—

35

That curriculum I provided—
Are only the fringe benefits
Not her whole take from me, by any means.
This much I'm sure of: She met people here of a sort
That would not have swum into her ken
Without my providing them—
And never would have noticed her existence
Except she was attached to me.
And it's people, isn't it
She claims to set such store by nowadays—
Not art, not literature, not learning.
It's humanity she's so great on now, isn't it?
Now, that is to say, that she knows all
She thinks one needs to know of what I know
Or knows all of it, say I, she's capable of taking in.

It was beautiful watching her learn. At first
I thought she might herself do something serious.
(I always think so.)
We read aloud in all the good languages (live or dead)
And loved each other in them—and out of them—right
    along.

*"Per più fiati gli occhi ci sospinse
quella lettura, e scolorocci il viso—"*

"Even when you don't understand it," I used to say to
    her,
"You can enjoy the sound of it."
Looking back, I feel she understood it all—
Almost at once. All too well. She was *very* quick.
But she enjoyed nothing. *That*, in the end,
Is what I had above all else to teach her.

There were certain complications.
(There always are)
I *wanted* her to like my friends
And make them hers
Even when it meant their liking me less
And turning on me—some of them—toward the last.
I wanted her to like them,
For how could she feel anything for what we read
When she had had no life of her own
That mattered.
I wish all the world could have seen her
When I first brought her here to stay
(Nobody could believe I was serious at first)
Or, better still, the day she first turned up
In my classroom—I was doing a stint of lecturing
Out in Cincinnati. Seven lectures, free
To all comers, and with enough money in it for me
To live the rest of the year on.
She said things in the question periods there
That made me see that *anything, everything*
Might be possible where there was such innocence.
I saw she was *intelligent*. And I could tell
That nobody else in the room
Could tell she was. She had read
All the wrong things.
The wrong poems, the wrong novels, the wrong quarter-
  lies.
But something about the way she didn't mind learning
They were the wrong ones
Made me see her possibilities.
It wasn't just her reading that was misguided, though.
She was *fat* and chewed gum and wore amethyst earrings
And didn't know that it mattered
Didn't even know it mattered she was obese.
I couldn't really blame my friends

For being slow to believe in her. She was not
Prepossessing. Not to their eyes.
But that's the kind of girl I'm often
Taken with, attracted to. I'm apt to like her
For all she's not but *could* be—
Given, of course, understanding and affection
Given inspiration
—From the right person.

      My friends did finally like her.
They saw her transformed before their eyes.
Partly, I suppose, they liked her just for that,
Out of a kind of appreciation for the miracle
And partly, I think, because they were happy to see
I could *still* inspire such love and such change
In a young girl.
They took her places in the City
I don't go to any more
Showed her things
I don't care about any more.
There was a general satisfaction all round, I think,
With the way things were, and were becoming.
She gave entertainments of a most delightful sort—
A costume party at Hallowe'en
And again a masquerade at New Year's.
She got me up in costumes
No one could recognize me in
(She covered my bald head with a wild boy's wig).
On other occasions she gave me roles to play
I did not know I was fitted for.
I carved a duck, I drank too much wine, I danced.
One would have thought I was her age,
Though when I *was* her age, I did not like that at all.
She made my old friends seem better friends.

She introduced new people into our circle—
People of a sort I had not known I could enjoy:
Politicians and show people of a kind
Who have intellectual pretensions.
And in the summer
When we all moved to the Vineyard
She filled my cottage there with houseguests
And kept them quiet till afternoon.
Why, I was actually happy to see them there, too,
When I emerged from my morning's work in my study.
I emerged from my study an affable old me
Nobody knew existed.
In the end, they said *I* had changed
Even more than she had.

    The difference was,
Nobody knew how much *she* had changed.
When she first came to me
She hardly knew how to let me
Put an arm about her waist.
One night I showed her herself in the mirror.
She had no clothes on and was by then
As slender as anyone wants any woman to be.
When I said, "That's you," she looked at herself
In astonishment.
And from that moment she was mine.
The life we knew from that moment
Was something one doesn't put down even
In one's journal. (Which, after all, one keeps only for posterity.)
And from that moment
The work I did, mornings in my study,
Was almost beyond belief.
At the end of a morning I'd look back over my pages

In wonder.
I could hardly believe it was me.

  But the general satisfaction all round
Is what makes for difficulty now the end of it's come.
It is over, that's all, so far as I can see.
There is nothing more in it—not for me.
But others won't have it so—some of my friends, that is—
Those who have been understanding of me before
Come asking how I can do such a thing.
I laugh in their faces.
To myself I say,
"Well, let her have those friends she's made through me—
I've some to spare—
If that's what she's after."
And I tell *them* so—everybody.
I can hardly count the friends she sets upon me
Pleading privately, sometimes drunkenly,
On the telephone, and usually after midnight,
Or even denouncing me in print, some of them,
In places it makes me laugh to see my name.
They tell me I treat her like a student.
That I treat all my lovers so and that it must stop now.
I say, "Of *course* I do. They *are* my students.
They *learn* from me. Don't you recall
How much she had to learn when she came?"
And they say, reproachfully, that there must already be someone else
For me to behave so.
I say, "Of *course* there is."
I say, "Isn't there always?
Didn't I push someone else out of the nest for her?
And now it's time for her to move over.
I can't help it if I'm the kind of man I am," I tell them.

"It's what artists are like.
Doesn't everybody know that?"

2. An old letter, found posthumously among her possessions

Dearest Maud,
    You must not write me here again.
Now that I've lost so much weight
And look the perfect slut for him
He suspects everyone of being "in love" with me.
He has me watched constantly by his "trusted friends,"
The literary toadies who surround him.
If he suspected for one moment
This body of mine had ever been touched before
—Especially by a female of the species—
He'd throw me out on my ear.
Or maybe he'd keep me here and do worse.
You wouldn't believe . . . Well, anyway,
He knows an immense amount about everything, includ-
    ing sex,
As you used to say you "bet" he did.
And I have learned and learned and learned.
First thing you know I'll be dropping French
And Italian phrases in my letters.
The trouble is he still keeps back
What we've really wanted from him, darling.
And I doubt sometimes he'll ever give himself away.
I mean I doubt sometimes that he *could* if he would.
For I don't think he knows how he does it—or, rather,
    did it.
His art—as I see it now—and as you've always suspected—
Has nothing to do with anything else in his life.

    At any rate, you must not write me here again.
It was a harebrained scheme of yours sending me here

In the first place, for our purposes.
Who else but you, dearest, could have devised
A scheme so underhanded or so daring or so wicked?
Sometimes when he talks of having "discovered" me
In that classroom in Cincinnati
I can hardly keep from laughing in his face.
Yes, I am very much aware, my dearest friend,
That my sleuthing here was supposed to take six weeks
And not the two years I've already stretched it to.
But I must tell you frankly
That though I haven't unearthed the answer
To our literary riddle,
I have found something else I like.

It's the life here I like, and I don't mean
To give it up. Moreover, I cannot say too often
That your letters are the only immediate threat
To what I have. You *must not* write me here again.
You might spoil everything.
And you must not do that if—
If you know what's good for you, my love.
That sounds too crude and too harsh
But I want to impress upon you
Before you send another of your berating letters
That I've found something more than literary treasure here,
Something more than the germ of his creativity
Which you and I thought we could do a book about.
I know you will say to yourself: "It's him!
She's fallen for him!"
It's not true, my only one.
Oh, God, if you only knew how dull he is,
How bald he is, how active his bladder, how inactive his
    bowels,
And how he bores me . . . in bed.

The source of his art, I must confess,
Is buried too deep for me to fathom.
Those poems you used to read aloud to me,
Those poems that made him a world celebrity
Cannot truly be credited to him
But only to that mysterious person
Whose death inspired them, whoever she was
—Some girl he knew, perhaps only slightly, in his adoles-
cence.
Or some boy. Who knows?
There have been moments in bed
When I thought there was reason to suspect just that!

I often think how right your intuition was
When it told you he would like to find me plain
So he could make me beautiful,
That he would like to find me ignorant
So he could educate me.
It's changing someone he likes.
And I suppose that's to be found in the poems,
Though I can't read them any more.
No more can he, so far as I can tell!
When he reads to us
It's always from his theorizing essays
About art and literature and language.
And he cares nothing about any of that.
Not really. Not in the way one does when one is young.
It's all theory with him.
None of it means anything.
(Not even bed means anything to him)
Or has anything to do with those verses you love so.
I remember your longing to know
How the man who wrote that poetry in his youth
Could waste the rest of his life

Writing those dull essays, those endless analyses.
Well, it's his essays he's like when you know him.
His talk is eternally of his opinionated, analyzing self.
Those around him and all the rest of the world, for that
    matter,
May say his essays are brilliant and his talk is brilliant
But it is only a case of the emperor's-new-clothes.
He's *so* dull.
From time to time I've found a chance
To take a hurried peek into his journals
(When he was away and careless where he left his keys)
And the journals, I assure you, are as crudely written,
As pretentious, as self-deceiving
And as self-inflating and as dull
As all his talk and all his other proseyfying of recent years.

But still, my darling, when all is said,
He *does* have his emperor's new clothes
To wear. No one dares deny him that.
And I begin to wonder if
After a certain time in life
There is anything better, anything more comforting
Than having the emperor's new clothes to wear.
Once they are yours, they are something
People are less likely to take away from you
Than anything else. People are such cowards and such
    fools.
There is no one in the world, I think—
No one in his literary world, at any rate—
That would ask the terrible, ruinous question
Of a man of his reputation.
What is more—
And this is what you must consider, my old friend—
He has convinced the whole world,

Himself included,
That I am charming, gracious, beautiful, brilliant.
Nobody who matters dare think otherwise.
And so I have my own
Empress's new clothes to wear
Which I won't willingly give up.
I am the darling of his court—of his coterie, others call it.
Everyone wants to be seen with me everywhere.
Everyone wants my opinion on everything.
Because I am nearest to the throne.
Well, can't you see? You ought to see.
If one cannot be Emperor,
Then this is the next best thing.
And don't you see? You ought to see.
It is not for him I want to stay on here.
But for the place he gives me in the sun.
It's fame of a sort, or feels like fame.
You've warned me sufficiently
That he will tire of me one day
As he has of the others.
I know. I know. I know.
I have lain awake nights, thinking just that.
Oh, I know.
And yet if only I could make him love me
As he once loved
The unnamed person of the poems!
Then this would never end.
How would that be possible, I ask myself
(Because when you've tasted what I've tasted—
Fame or near fame—it's bitter to give it up),
How would it be possible?
It was the *death* of that person, wasn't it,
Which inspired
His deepest feelings of love?
And so, unless I die, he cannot love me forever.

Well, if it's only in death I can keep my place,
If that's the only way.
That at least it's food for thought
When we have our little quarrels, he and I.

Dearest, don't regret your loss of me
When it's you I'd love still
If I could love anyone but myself—myself famous.
And don't pity me for what may lie ahead.
I am happy, happy.
But, love, you must not write me here again.

3. An entry in his journal

It was an accident.
Of that we can all be certain.
She made the wrong turn on the road, that's all.
It was a road she didn't know as well
As she thought she did.
—Not untypical of her, I have to say.
She hadn't been to the Poconos in the five years
Since we were there together.
How could she be expected to remember
Those twisting little mountain roads
That seem to drop off into nowhere
And *do* if you don't watch yourself.
No one has said to *me* it *wasn't* an accident,
And I know she would have left a note
Or shown some sign of her intention
If her act had been directed at me.
Still, the thought occurs—the possibility.
But I tell myself that even she
In her recent morbid state of mind
Would not have done such an awful thing to *me*.

The people she had been staying with
At Poconos Pines, tried to keep her from setting out
At night. But she insisted she liked to drive at night,
That she did her best thinking then.
She had had a quiet day that day, they say.
Had hardly mentioned my name.
No hysterics, no histrionics of any kind.
Just before setting out she did recite some lines
From an old poem of mine that she had memorized
Before she had ever set eyes on me.
But she went on from that, they say, to talk of other
   things,
Yawning and stretching before the fire
In her very natural way
And having one more cup of coffee for the road.
She had most of her possessions with her in the car she'd
   rented.
Among the few effects she had left behind
In her efficiency at the Chelsea
(I hadn't known that's where she had set up)
Were a dozen or so books, odd bits of clothing,
And some old letters and scribblings of her own
(Which, under the circumstances, they very properly de-
   stroyed).
Nothing else—no note or letter relevant to the tragedy.
No accusations of me.

   It was one of those unfortunate accidents, that's all,
Made worse for the rest of us
By the circumstances.
Made worse for me, moreover,
And given a special irony
Because someone else whom I once loved,
And who loved me every bit as much

As she, did take his own life
And made it seem an accident—
Took his own life, I mean, because of me.

I was a young boy in my early teens,
Hardly more than a child,
Though of course *not* a child any longer.
And he was younger by only a few months.
Or was it older? Since our acquaintance
Lasted only a matter of weeks, there is really more
That I don't know about him than that I know.
Our friendship was of so intense a kind
That we did not ask questions about the other's life.
We had both so recently discovered our bodies, our minds,
Our talents—our souls, it seemed to us—
That nothing else seemed worth our talking of.

And finally he killed himself for love of me.
How else is one to say it? Of course
It's not as simple or as beautiful as that,
But that's about how I wrote down my recollection of it
In my journal some years back. Only tonight
In the wake of her death
Did I go and look up the old entry.
I had some trouble finding it,
It was so brief. What struck me
Was how coldly I had recorded the old facts
(They were old even then when I decided
To put them in my journal). And I was struck
By how much better
I seem to remember it all now than I did then.
But perhaps the strangest part
Is that sometime in the intervening years
Or perhaps at the very time of writing it

(I have no recollection of doing so)
I had circled the passage with red pencil.
In fact, without that circling of the pencil
I don't know how I might ever have found the passage
There among the vast sheaf of papers
Which I keep locked away
From the eyes of all the world
In my study files.

How he died and why
Is not something that could be told
In the few declarative sentences I gave to it
Twenty years ago. But I was right
To try to do it that way. My poetry was all written then.
I knew there would be no more. I knew
I must forget that boy and forget that night he died.
But what a revelation it is
—Through this poor girl's sad death—what a revelation
That I have not forgotten the old hidden facts,
The old facts I so neatly skirted in my poems.

The confidences he and I shared,
The intimacy we had were like none
I had known before in my life. To think
There was someone else, and that another boy in my own
    school,
Who shared my foolish dream of becoming someday
A great artist of one kind or another!
It made the games we had to play after class hours
In that old-fashioned Latin school
Seem like real games and altogether a joy to play
When we could look at each other from opposing sides
And wink at each other and know what we knew.

It was at Class Day Exercises, in early May,
That the thing happened.
There was a banquet that night in the refectory.
We sang the school songs
And sang some parodies that I myself had made up.
But to the two of us the Exercises all seemed hogwash.
I don't know which of us had the idea first,
But we slipped out long before the alma mater was called
    for.
It was a warm night. "Let's go swimming," he said,
"In the reservoir."
We went on tiptoe
Under the lighted windows of the gym,
And then on through the dark lane
Under the linden trees. Suddenly he stopped.
He looked away into the dark as though he had heard
Or seen something. But I could tell somehow
It wasn't that. When he looked back at me
His eyes were full to the brim with tears.
"What's the matter?" I asked.
"It's only," he said, "that I think you are so wonderful."
I drew away, but he seized both my hands and held them
    in his grasp.
"I love you," he said.
"Don't say that," I protested, trying to draw my hands
    free.
Before I could understand his intention really, he had
    leaned
Forward and kissed me on the mouth.
"You queer!" I shouted and spat into his face.
At just that moment I think he saw the master
Who must have followed us from the refectory
And who now stood watching.
And then he turned and he ran, and I raced after him.
I'm not sure whether I meant

To pummel him with my fists
Or tell him it was all right.
At any rate, the master called to us by name
And presently I turned back.
Oh God, I wish I had not.
I never saw him again.
They searched the woods for him half the night
And found his body in the reservoir the next morning.
He had dived, by accident they said, into the shallow end.

    What *might* he have become if he had lived?
What turn might our friendship
Or our love have taken?
In the days that followed it seemed to me sometimes
That it might easily have been myself
Who made that advance
For surely, somehow or other, in some way or other,
I loved him no less than he loved me.
It seemed to me he might well have spat into my face.
And it might have been me
Who was found floating in the reservoir.
Instead, I was left in the silence
Which my elders placed about me.
The master walked me back to the refectory that night
Without a word passing between us.
Never afterward was my friend's name
Ever spoken in my presence—
Not by my teachers, my parents, or even my classmates.
But I kept him alive in my imagination
Thinking each year, as I grew up and became a man,
How he would be then if he had lived,
How he and I would have loved
Or liked each other.
Ten years later when I began to write my poems to him

I had, in my perversity, to turn him into a woman.
I had, in fact, long since turned him into a woman in my
    mind.
Something had happened that night in the linden path
That made it my necessity to speak of love only to women.
All other possibilities were that night cut off from me.
I have said in print somewhere
"The heroine of my poems
Is a creature of my imagination."
So she is. The heroines
Of all our love affairs are that.
We must create creatures whom we can love.
Else I do not know what love is.

    And tonight I have brought a new girl
To live with me here in the apartment over Central Park.
In June she'll no doubt go with me to the Vineyard.
She is very decent-looking.
She possesses a superior mind.
But she doesn't know how to walk across a room.
She walks like a boy
And begins each sentence she utters with
"Like" or "I mean."
She's as young as that.
No one thinks that I shall have her with me
For very long.
They don't see so clearly as I
What her potentiality is,
How graceful and how well-spoken
And how altogether feminine
She will become
Before she and I are through.

The Throughway

THEY WERE A COUPLE WHO HAD LIVED AL-
ways in the same house since they had first married—not
one they owned but one they had been able to rent all
through the years. The house was in an old section of the
city, the very part of town in which they both had grown
up. Once upon a time it had been a fashionable section, of
course, but even when Harry and Isabel were young people
it was considered no more than highly respectable and
"comfortable." Yet they had been delighted to go on living
there and had taken satisfaction in bringing up their two
daughters in the neighborhood where they had themselves
been young. When the daughters married and left them to
go and live in the suburbs, they were happy to continue
living there alone.

Harry's work was nearby. Just two blocks away there was
a cluster of stores where Isabel liked to do all her shopping
for the house. Having everything so close, they had not
found it necessary to own a car—not necessary or feasible.
Harry's work had never amounted to more than holding
down a job at the wire-mesh plant, but living always where
they did and as they did, they had never suffered any real
hardship. Isabel was an excellent manager. As for Harry,
there was no kind of repair job about the place that he
couldn't do for himself. He even installed a new furnace
when the old one wore out. Their contemporaries had all

prospered more than they had, of course, and had moved into the newer developments farther out in the east end. But these same contemporaries often expressed envy for Harry and Isabel's lot in life. Everyone said that they were such sane and sensible and unsuperficial people. . . . In a changing, uncertain world it was good to know a couple who enjoyed such stability.

But this was how it was for Harry and Isabel before the unfortunate business about the throughway came up. After that—after it was announced that one leg of the new throughway way system, connecting all the outlying sections of the growing city, would come down their very street and require demolition of their entire block— everything seemed different. Through certain connections that Harry had—boyhood friends in high places—he managed to obtain a court hearing in which to make his protest against the route the throughway was taking. From that day he revealed himself to all the world as nothing more than a local crank. His friends could no longer enjoy dropping by his house for an evening of relaxed talk about old times. And from about that time Isabel, out of embarrassment perhaps, since she clearly did not share her husband's obsession, began to decline all invitations from even her oldest acquaintances.

Worse still, from that day forward Harry and Isabel seemed almost strangers to each other. At times it was difficult for either of them to understand the motive behind anything the other did or said. On the other hand, there were as many times when each would suspect that he or she understood the other's motives only too well! The routing of the new throughway, which was considered to be in the public interest, seemed to have undermined that very serenity for which Harry and Isabel were envied. On the day scheduled for their removal from the old house, they met in the downstairs hall not as two who were allied against an intruding world but as two adversaries.

Isabel had left her room and come downstairs half an hour before Harry did. Finally she heard him shuffling about on the bare floor in his room and in the upstairs hall. Then she heard him on the stairs. She went into the hall and waited at the foot of the stairs, just outside the living-room doorway. He descended the stairs as though he didn't see her there at the bottom. Finally he stopped on the last step and looked over her head into the dismantled living room. "Three moves," he said quietly, smiling faintly, vaguely—still not looking at her, "three moves are equal to one burning. That's how the old saying goes, isn't it?"

Though she stood with her back to the living room, Isabel could see its whole jumble and disarray and even the terrible, blank bareness of its walls, all reflected in the wounded-animal look on Harry's face. Why, he looked like a man nearly eighty this morning instead of like one nearly sixty. She kept thinking that somehow she ought to feel guilty about it. But she could not take the blame. She could not find where her fault lay. In his eyes she seemed to see the goldfish bowl on the mantelpiece directly behind her— almost literally she felt she could see it—and she saw in the expression about his mouth the canary's cage with its night cover still on to keep the little thing from taking fright when the movers should arrive. And as Harry's eyes roved slowly about the room behind her, it seemed to her that she could even see the drops of cold rain batting against the curtainless, shadeless windows. "I read in the paper recently," she heard him saying now, his eyes still directed toward the living room as though he were speaking to the covered birdcage or the fishbowl, "I read in the paper that one-third of this country's population moves every year."

Suddenly Isabel reached out and placed a hand on his

sweater sleeve. She left it there a moment, thinking surely it would make him look at her. In that moment it seemed that his not looking at her during the past weeks had been what hurt her most. Presently, in a tone so dispirited and soft that he may not have noticed that she had spoken, she asked, "How can you even want to stay on here?" Then, as though unexpectedly receiving new energy and a new inspiration, she went on, "Why, last winter the water got up in the basement till it ruined those two old chests of drawers you were refinishing. Didn't you even mind that? And, Harry, we are in for another wet, rainy fall. It's hardly September and the rain already coming down like October!"

Still looking past her, as if addressing someone over her shoulder, he said, "That's why I fired up the furnace this morning." As he spoke, the furnace pipes rattled and clanged as though there were a prison riot in progress.

"Yes, and *that* furnace! Listen to it! And you, at your age, down there shoveling coal at five a.m. A *coal* furnace!"

"I don't know why you should disparage the furnace," he said. And now it was as though he were talking to her—or to someone—over the telephone. "It's a good furnace still," he said in a loud, heartfelt tone. "Hardly four years old. Besides, I like knowing there's a real fire down there—not just some gas piped in, and a jet."

He was silent a moment. Then he fixed his eyes on her for the first time. "It isn't natural," he said, "for a woman to care so little about her home."

Except for the tone of his voice when he said that, she might have thought he was out of his senses. And his gaze on her was suddenly so intense and honest she could almost believe that what he said made sense. . . . After a moment she began shaking her head from side to side. That was all she could do now. Here it was Monday morning, the day of the move, and he was still saying that sort of thing to her. What did he mean? And how dare he? It was really too much. He had been no help at all. He had taken no part in the packing or in finding a new place. All weekend he had wandered about the house like a sick animal who only *sensed* there was going to be a change, padding about in his soft-soled slippers, with never a word to anybody, and never once offering to lend a hand. Their two sons-in-law had had to come in and shift the crates and barrels about for her.

AT LAST HARRY TURNED AWAY INTO THE hall. He was heading for the dining room, she guessed—as though they could eat in *there* this morning! "What isn't natural," she began, not knowing what she was going to say, but following after him and determined to say something, "what's not natural is for a *man* to care so much about a house—especially a house that isn't his." She was willing to say the worst kind of thing that might pop into her head this morning if it took that to prevent Harry's falling back into yesterday's silence.

In the dining-room doorway he halted again, almost as if he had found her confronting him in that doorway too. Instead, she was so close behind him that when he stopped her nose actually touched the coarse texture of his cardigan. And she didn't need to peer over the stooped shoulders or around his straight-hanging sweater arms to make out what it was he had come up against that stopped him. She knew the kind of disorder the dining room was in. She could see right through him—she could see it with *his* eyes—the dark table laid with cartons of kitchen junk instead of with the china and silver he expected, or wanted to expect. Then for a moment she had a clear vision, *his* vision, of the heavy oak dining table set with their white bone china (which she had used every day since they set up housekeeping, without ever breaking even one cup handle) and their wedding silver (which she had never spared, never saved for company, but which she had polished every Saturday night and had used and enjoyed every day that came, just the way he wanted her to). The vision of their table all properly set for breakfast with the cut-glass sugar bowl and cream pitcher, *his* vision, was so vivid to her that she closed her eyes and kept them closed for a moment, trying to free herself of it. . . . It was never easy for her not to see things the way he saw them or the way he wanted her to see them.

Her eyes were still shut when she heard him suddenly laugh out loud. It wasn't a kind of laughter she had ever thought him capable of. Without opening her eyes she stretched out an arm in her self-imposed darkness, reaching for him with her open hand. But now he was no longer within her reach.

It was still worse when she looked. Harry had crossed the room and dropped down into one of the straight chairs at the table, just as though the table were properly set, dropped down into his own chair, and was smiling at her across the litter on the table in that new way he had that seemed more alien than his laughter.

"Dear Harry!" she said under her breath.

Harry put his two hands on the table and spoke with a casual warmth, as though he were merely asking what favorite dish of his he could expect this morning. "What would you have me care about instead?" he asked. There was something almost chipper in his voice. "That is, if I am not to care about our home." His voice sounded so natural that she forgot all restraint and let her anger come back.

"Why, you ought to care about your work, that's what!" (*Now* what was she saying to him? she asked herself.)

"I do," he said.

"You never have!"

She wondered at her own fierceness. She was saying things she couldn't have said to him six weeks before—before the hearing and its attendant publicity began. It was as if she had picked up the hateful, insinuating tone of the city officials and the lawyers and mixed it with the rudeness of the reporters. She heard herself, and she wanted to stop her ears to shut out her own voice.

"I've liked my work just as much as any man does," he said. "So leave that out, if you please. Stick to your real complaint, which is that I've liked my home a great deal better than most men do!"

"But this isn't *our* house—or *your* house. It's a house we've *rented*. Our furniture's our only real home, Harry. And we're taking that with us, Harry."

"Oh," he said, "so you hold that against me then, do you—that we've always only rented. Yet you have always maintained you didn't mind." Now it was he who sounded like the lawyers at the hearing.

"You know better, Harry. I haven't minded—not for myself." She had now followed him all the way into the dining room and stood with her hands clasped and resting on the skirt of her starched apron.

"Anyway," he said, "it's a house we've rented long enough to feel pretty much at home in. Thirty-one years. Our children grew up here, Isabel . . . I mean to die here."

"You're still saying that? *Today*?"

Now he had frightened her.

Her fright seemed like something new to her, and yet it seemed familiar too. Momentarily she turned her eyes inward and asked herself, had she been frightened of him always? Frightened of dear, gentle Harry? Harry, who had wanted only to have his peace and keep out of the world's way? But yes, that was it. It was not the throughway that was the cause of their distress. It was Harry's drawing away from life. All through the years, really, he had only been waiting for the throughway, even wishing for it in his own way, wanting to be cornered. He simply could not have borne it if they had suddenly rerouted the throughway down some other street than theirs! . . . Again she shook her head. Such thoughts! She pushed one of the straight chairs over opposite him and sat down. "Listen, my husband, my dearest, we've always known we'd have to move someday. We've loved it here, but this neighborhood—this whole end of town—was going down when we married. That's how it happened we were able to rent so cheaply here where we did."

"I wanted to rent here," he said grimly. "It was not just something we could afford—not for me."

"I know."

"I grew up in this end of town, Isabel. So did you. Why not die here? Everybody has the right to die where he's—"

"I'm not thinking of dying, Harry!" she cried. It was as though she were fighting off the sudden image of death itself. "And you shouldn't be." Presently she bent forward and narrowed her eyes at him. "I . . . don't . . . believe . . . you . . . are, Harry."

"But I am, somehow," he said.

"Why, I don't care where I die," she said recklessly. Her two plump forearms were planted on the table before her, and she could feel goose-bumps rising on them. "Isn't it enough just to go on being alive? No matter where it is? Isn't our love anything at all to you any more?" But at once she felt she had spoken the word "love" exactly as she would have spoken the name of a long-dead child. And she was so shocked by what she had said, and how she had said it, that she drew in her breath sharply.

At first Harry didn't seem to have heard her. Then presently he said: "But *here!*" He was smiling that new smile again. His mouth turned up at the corners, like a child's drawing. "*Here* in the end of town where we grew up and spent our lives! I tell you, I mean to go on firing that furnace of mine to the end, Isabel. I've talked myself into a queer corner, I know. I stop sometimes and ask myself why I've done it. But I can't give in. Can't you see?"

Harry got up from his chair and went to the dining room's plate-glass front window. Stripped of its draperies and its net curtains and even its green canvas shade, it was bare like a store window. How efficiently she had *un*done everything, he said to himself. Just as efficiently and economically as she had always *done* everything. He could imagine her saying to herself: Why leave anything behind in a house that is going to be pulled down? She would have soaked the wallpaper off the walls if she had deemed it practical. And she was so sure she could set them up just as cozily somewhere else. It was her great pride that she could make something of nothing. And that was the trouble. She had made their nothing such a great plenty. She had never allowed him to feel poor, to feel himself a nobody. But he had *wanted* to feel himself a nobody, to know that he was poor. He had needed to need. It seemed to him that from that he would have derived his deepest satisfaction. Long ago, before they were married even, she and he had talked a great deal about "accepting the world." But he saw now how differently they had meant it. When, last year, they had heard the first threats that the throughway might come down their street, he saw that she seemed almost to welcome the idea. He had suspected her at times of having intercourse with the enemy. He smiled at the expression. The enemy, in his mind, had become the old friend from whom he had rented the house these thirty-one years—the old friend at first, that is, then his widow, then his widow's heirs. It seemed quite possible that Isabel might have gone to the heirs and urged them not to fight the plan—to their heirs and perhaps the other property owners too. Her way of accepting the worst was to welcome it, to invite it, to be for it, of it. Just within recent months she had conveniently discovered all that was wrong with the old house and how bad it was for his heart that he had to fire that furnace. Or had she hated every bit of it all along? Was the throughway only what she had been waiting for?

He stood looking out into the rain. The rain seemed to have subsided somewhat. Out in the wet street a car went by, then a truck. But nobody passed on the sidewalk. There wasn't another house in the block that hadn't been vacated. Two across the street had already come down; even the rubble had been cleared away.

Now she moved up beside him at the window. He felt her hand on his sleeve again. "We'd best get a bite of breakfast in the kitchen, Harry," she said. "The vans are due at eight o'clock."

He answered her in a whisper: "They've widened this street every ten years since we've been living here, Isabel. The trees went, the grass went next—now the people." While he spoke, a gray cat out in the rain went scurrying along the sidewalk on the other side of the street. "Hurry, puss!" he said in a normal voice. Then he added, "It's a funny thing. I had a dream about a cat last night. I thought I saw a mother cat eating its kittens. . . . We had one who did that when I was a boy."

Isabel made no response immediately. The two of them continued to stand at the window, looking out at the empty lots across the street with the gaping holes that had once been basements. Presently her hand fell away from his arm, but he could tell she was still there even before she spoke. "Harry, don't begin again. You've said it all. You've said it to *everybody*. That should satisfy you. The lawyer tried to make you understand, even after the judge couldn't. I thought maybe he had. Till this weekend, I did. You're a man and ought to understand it better than I do. We're out of character in this, both of us. I've never had any thought but to be what you wanted me to be. My one desire in life has been to give in to you—"

"Yes, that's true."

"—and make you comfortable and live within your—within our—means."

"That's true."

"I've never had any thoughts of my own, Harry."

"I know."

"You've always told me what to think, and I've thought it. But, Harry, even I can understand that it's only the property owners who might have stopped the throughway, and they didn't want to. You ought to have known it was hopeless when *they* hung back. Your own lawyer said you ought to have your head examined for making such a useless fuss just because you could. He said so to me, in just so many words. It's nothing to smile over, either—especially not like that. *I'd* think you were crazy, too, if I didn't know the truth. It isn't the house, Harry, and it isn't the part of town you care so much about. Why, this part of town's changed beyond recognition. It's the throughway you hate for itself—or love for itself—coming down our street instead of the next street, or the next. You hate it, or love it, because you always knew it or something like it would come, had to come. . . . But it's not our street really, Harry. It's those people's street who owned these old houses if it's anybody's, and they didn't even stand by you when you got it into court."

"Is ownership the only thing in life? Can't you have a right to something without owning it?" He didn't look around at her. He went on looking out the window. Outside the rain had begun to fall more heavily again. "I own nothing," he whispered. "I made up my mind early in life to ask for nothing. I thought that nothing was something they could never take away from me. But now it seems that isn't so. The world today wants your nothing, even. Perhaps it always did."

"Harry, don't begin that again. Not with that smile, anyway. I have to tell you, Harry, it does scare me a little to have you whispering and smiling so strangely. It would scare anyone. It's strange enough seeing the house like this. It's been strange enough living in this empty street all these weeks and months. Oh, you might as well know it now: I've been scared a long time living in this neighborhood."

"You wanted to be scared in this neighborhood. You wanted to want to move."

"Last winter, for instance, when you worked overtime so many nights at the plant, I used to hear noises at these downstairs windows."

"You wanted there to be noises at the windows."

"At least once I *knew* it was someone trying to break in. . . . Don't smile so, Harry. . . . Some nights I almost telephoned one of the girls to send her husband over; but I didn't want to worry them any more than you. Yes, I switched on those outside lights you've put up. I suppose that's all that stopped whoever it was. But I've even been scared in the daytime here. For years, Harry. And since all the neighbors left—*such* neighbors as they were, too, toward the last! Oh, Harry, we've always known we'd have to move sometime! Even if they'd put the throughway farther east, it wouldn't have been a year before the Blacks would have been in this block. They're already just two doors the other side of the Cass Street intersection."

"I don't mind the Negroes any more," he said.

"I know you don't mind them. And they'll be everywhere before long. You say it's right. A sign of progress, you say. Well, the throughway is a sign of progress, isn't it? How can you be for progress and against it, too?"

"I can, somehow," he said. She parted her lips to speak,

but he interrupted. "And I've reached a point where it's no use trying to explain things."

"Then there's no use my saying more," she said resignedly. "It's seven-thirty, Harry. The vans—"

"Forget the vans," he said sharply. He turned his face to her, and they looked coldly into each other's eyes for a moment. "The van's aren't coming, Isabel," he said finally.

Isabel smiled at him with an indulgent expression. "The vans *are* coming, Harry," she said patiently, as though explaining something to a child—explaining it for perhaps the second or third time. "It's all arranged for, dear. They'll be here at eight—rain or shine."

"No," he said. "I telephoned the transfer company from the plant on Friday. The van's aren't coming."

"You *wouldn't* have, Harry!" she wailed.

"I told them their men would have me to deal with if they showed up here."

"Harry, you *didn't*! Not without consulting me! . . . And letting me go through this weekend."

"And you know how they'd feel about dealing with a crazy fellow like me, after all they've seen in the papers."

"Then I've done all I can do in this house, Harry."

"There's not *much* more anyone can do," her husband answered.

"Not *much* more?" she asked, lifting her eyes suddenly to his.

"Not much more," he said.

IT WAS ONLY THEN SHE REALIZED HOW tired she was—not tired from the packing up, or tired even from the incessant ringing of the telephone or the being stopped by strangers on the street or by reporters waiting to take her picture, wanting *her* picture—*hers!*—the last resident, the wife of the man who said the throughway shouldn't come down this street, wanting *her* picture doing *her* last shopping in the old-timey, pint-sized kind of Piggly-Wiggly store that they still had in their neighborhood. She wasn't tired from the aggressive resentment that other people showed for someone who thought he could stop the throughway. No, what she was tired out by was fighting with herself to keep herself from fighting him. All these years, more than anything else, she had wanted him to have his own gentle way in everything, his own peace. That was what she had believed. She had laughed with him whenever he was passed over for promotion at the plant, and said with him, What did it matter? How could it change their life? Didn't they already have their own little niche? But she knew now what it mattered. She knew now that in this day and age either you accepted the world, manifested yourself to the world, let the world have its way with you, or one way or another, sooner or later, directly or indirectly, you must pay its price—your peace. Yes, sooner or later it would come down your street. But, oh, actually she knew now that so far as she was concerned Harry was part of the world, that he was part of what was not her, that is, and knew that in the end everybody was part of it except yourself. Time was when she believed she kept herself from fighting him because it was the womanly, wifely thing to do. Or had she ever believed that, really? Wasn't it that she had really known all along that in his meekness he was far stronger and more willful than she and would never yield an inch to her in any struggle there might ever be between them? His self-righteous withdrawal from the contest of life she saw now not as a negative thing but as a positive force pulling her with it toward a precipice somewhere. But she had to try to save herself. She could not let him drag her over the precipice. . . . Suddenly she left him at the window, and went hurriedly from the room.

HARRY DIDN'T KNOW WHERE SHE HAD GONE
until he heard the rattle of the metal coat-hanger on the
floor of the hall closet. It was an unmistakable sound. He
reminded himself that she would already have packed up
all the wooden coat-hangers—they cost *money*—and probably all the wire ones too, except one for his coat and one
for hers. And no doubt she had a place reserved in some
box or other for those two wire hangers even. No doubt
in some box—he thought it before he could stop himself,
before he could tell himself that it didn't make sense—no
doubt in some box she had a spot reserved for *him*. Perhaps
one of those boxes she had been saving in the attic through
the years had been for him all along. Ah, the good-natured
teasing he had done about her saving habits! It had seemed
such a funny little fault for her to have. And in fact it
ought to have put the fear of God in him long ago! He
ought to have seen it for what it was. While he had been
always avoiding the box the world wanted to put him in,
she had been preparing one for him in his own attic. All
that string and those old papers and boxes had been to
wrap *him* in! She had known the day would come. . . . But
what nonsense, he said to himself, trying to calm himself.
Am I really out of my head? What nonsense. Am I afraid
of such a reasonable, sensible, practical soul as Isabel? . . .
Nevertheless, it was just as well he had canceled the order
for the moving vans. In effect, she had been going to wrap
him up and carry him off with the rest of the furniture.
Then when she had moved him and the other furniture
out, *they* would come and pull the house down. He had
watched them tearing down the houses across the street.
He had not told her at the time, but that was when he first
realized he must do something. It was the wrong way for
those old houses to go. There was something indecent about
it, with those thugs hired to come in with their crowbars

and their cranes and their great, swinging mace-and-chains. It took murderers for that. Of course, as Isabel said, they were not *his* houses. No, but you couldn't watch without feeling it. Burning them would have been better—more decent. That's the way such old houses used to go. He could remember when a whole block on Spencer Avenue burned. There had been four houses in that block that were built before the Civil War. At least three generations had lived out their lives there. He remembered, too, when the old Milton house on Spruce Street burned. That was the house in which his parents had got married. When the block on Spencer Avenue burned, half the town had turned out to see it, and his father had been one of the volunteers who went in to help. When the Milton house burned, he remembered, his mother shed tears. He could remember also when the Dickinson house burned, the house in which his parents happened to be living when he was born. He had been a boy in his teens at the time of those fires. In those days nobody seemed ever to know how fires got started, and he could recall the strange feelings he used to have about it sometimes. . . . He couldn't understand now why he had had such feelings. . . .

Isabel came back into the dining room, slowly pulling on her lightweight cloth coat. From the window, he looked at her over his shoulder. "I'm going to one of the girls," she said. "You can find me when you've finally satisfied yourself. I've endured all I can, Harry. The thought of more publicity and more bickering with the city people is more than I can bear. You can do what you will about the furniture." (Suddenly he wondered if she had ever suspected that it might have been he trying to frighten her those nights when she was at home alone. He felt a flash of guilt, just as though it *had* been.) "Everything's packed up except a few dishes and things in the kitchen. I've written down the address of the new place on that barrel by the front door. It's Apartment A. It's on the first floor, Harry, as I've told you. There's a locker room in the basement that will hold all that won't go in the apartment. I've paid a month's rent in advance. . . . I'm going now. There's some breakfast for you in the kitchen if you can eat it."

She turned away abruptly and crossed the hall to the living room. The canary was chirping under its cover. She quickly removed the cover without looking at the bird. She couldn't bear to look at the poor, protected creature, so innocent and unsuspecting. From the mantel she took the package of seed and poured a full measure into the feeder. Replacing the package of seed on the mantel shelf, she glanced at the bowl of fish. The fish had always been considered mostly his. Beside the bowl lay a packet of fish food. It was open at one end, and she could see the white wafers inside. Somehow it looked repulsive to her. She stood gazing at the fish food, and afterward at the four little mottled fish, without ever lifting a hand. I have done all I can do here, she said to herself. It would take all the energy she had to propel herself through the doorway into the hall again and down the hall to the front door. She was not sure even that she could make that journey, but she knew her life depended upon it.

When she reached the center of the hall she saw that Harry had gone back to his chair at the table—the same chair he had sat in earlier. Her empty chair was still opposite him, across the layers of junk. He sat there smiling over at her chair.

"Whatever are you thinking, Harry?" she asked, despite herself. She had hoped to have spoken her last word.

He bent forward, putting his elbows on the edge of the table and resting his chin on the heels of his two hands. "Well, if you must know," he said, "I was thinking of the houses around here I saw burn when I was growing up."

Isabel's hand came up to her mouth. Behind her fingers,

under her breath, she uttered a little shriek. It was the cry of a small animal suddenly finding itself trapped when it thought it had escaped.

She wasn't even sure whether or not Harry heard her, because simultaneously she heard the radiators in the downstairs rooms begin to thump and hiss again. It seemed to her they were shaking the whole house. She saw Harry laugh soundlessly to himself.

"You know the houses I mean," he continued. "The old Milton house that the Thompsons lived in and where my parents were married, the Dickinson house, the houses in that block on Spencer Avenue." He paused and waited for one of the radiators, which had started up again, to become quiet. "It's a strange thing. It used to worry me that they never knew how those fires got started. Somehow I used to wonder if people thought *I* had done it. I even got so I had guilty feelings about it and half imagined that I *had* set the fires."

Slowly Isabel's hand fell from her mouth. Her lips parted, but for a moment she was speechless. . . . She saw at last! She understood! It seemed to her that she stood there for five minutes, or even longer, before she could speak or move. Then she said: "Harry, I understand, at last."

He rose from the table and put up one hand as though to ward off a blow. "No," he said. "No, you don't understand one bit!"

"But I do," she said. As she advanced toward him, he sat down at the table again. He tried to smile, but now the smile failed. He was looking at her with open hatred in his face.

"It's no use," he said.

"Harry, my darling, all along you've wanted *everything*, which is what everybody wants—not nothing. But something inside you made you feel that it was wrong."

"You won't ever understand," he said, looking again toward the front window. "You would have understood years ago if you were ever going to. It's not so simple that you can see it in a flash."

"It is. It is. It's just that you don't want me to see," she said furiously, all the tenderness gone from her voice. "You didn't want to see, yourself! But I do see now. And you see it yourself, Harry. Don't try to deceive me. You wouldn't have remembered those fires and how you felt about them except that suddenly you understood."

"No matter how you make me out or how you explain my coming to where I am, it doesn't alter anything," he said.

He rested his head on the chair back and closed his eyes. "I don't know whether I'm crazy or not. But if I'm not crazy, Isabel, we've something worse to face. If I'm not crazy, the rest of the world *is*." He opened his eyes and managed to smile at her. "It's as though ever since they widened that street out there the first foot—thirty years ago—as though I've known they would go on widening it till someday I wouldn't make sense about it. But there's no use our leaving here, Isabel. No matter where one goes—"

Isabel stopped listening and began wandering about the room as though she didn't know how to find her way out. She realized that they had only got back to where they began and that understanding didn't help. There was no help for them. She found herself standing in the wide doorway between the dining room and the hall. For a moment she leaned against the door jamb. Then, without consciously resolving to do so, she began letting herself down very easily and slowly to the floor. She sat with her legs spread out before her at such crooked angles that they looked broken. Harry got to his feet and came to her. But when he offered her his hand, she drew away from him.

"Don't do anything. I can't stop you."

"Isabel," he said impatiently. It was a tone she had never heard him use with her before. She sat on the floor gazing out into the hall and through the glass in the front door. She heard the clock upstairs striking eight. So the moving men *weren't* coming! And he *was* mad, of course. She couldn't doubt it now. Glancing down at her broken-looking legs, she found it unbearable to think that she would presently have to try to stand on them once more. And in that moment there seemed to pass before her eyes not the whole of her past life but rather the terrible eternity of life there seemed left before her. . . . Finally, as if in a dream, she saw one of Harry's frayed carpet slippers come down on the small area of floor between her own two feet, and then saw the other slipper lifted over her legs as he stepped over her and out into the hall. With her eyes and ears she followed his soft footsteps across the hall to the foot of the staircase and then down alongside the staircase to the door that led to the basement steps. She watched him place his hand on the polished brass knob. "Harry," she said in a hoarse voice, "what is it? What are you going down there for?"

"Nothing," he said, not looking back.

"Harry—"

"What is it?"

"Don't do anything. I can't stop you."

"Ah, Isabel, what are you suggesting?" He spoke in the same impatient tone as earlier, and she could see only the back of his head, which he held at an angle, as though straining to hear her. "What is it you wish I would do, Isabel?"

"Harry, I'm afraid of you." It was almost a direct appeal to him, he felt.

"You only *want* it to be me you have to be afraid of," he said.

"No, I *am* afraid of you."

She sat very rigid, as though hypnotized, and watched him open the door and place one foot on the first step of the basement stairs. Then she watched him begin to lift the other foot off the hall floor. It was as though instead of the length of the hall she were five or six inches from his foot. And as the heel of the slipper left the floor, though not yet the toe, she became aware of the ringing sound. The foot became aware of it, too, and the heel returned to the floor. The foot seemed to tell her it was the telephone out there in the back hall. The foot seemed to tell her who the caller would be, told her even before she raised her eyes to meet her husband's. Of course it would be one of the girls! And there was no not answering it. For if they did not answer, then the husband of one of the girls would leap into his car and, traveling the one already completed leg of the throughway, would arrive at their door within a matter of minutes. And if they did answer, it would no doubt bring the same son-in-law, because there would be no concealing that everything had gone wrong. Both of them knew that all decisions were, from that moment, over for them. To answer or not answer the telephone didn't matter. They were two old people who had behaved foolishly or who had almost behaved foolishly, and in the future all important decisions would be made for them. Henceforth they would be watched over and seen after. Henceforth they were in the hands of their children, and both of them asked silently, What other end would *not* have been better—more decent? Across the bare floor of the hall Harry and Isabel looked into each other's eyes with cold indifference. The past year, the past quarter-hour itself, seemed like a lifetime. And those long, peaceful years they had known together seemed but a short honeymoon at the beginning of their marriage, a brief interlude almost forgotten. . . . Who was that stranger standing awkwardly with one foot on the cellar stair? . . . Who was that odd-looking old woman crouched on the floor? . . . Why, it was she with whom he was trapped by circumstance to end his days. . . . Why, it was he with whom she must live out her life and whom she must no doubt nurse through a prolonged senility. . . . Ah, yes, ah, yes . . . a husband . . . a wife . . . a fellow human creature, anyhow . . . that the world had come in and estranged from one. What matter if it took a quarter of an hour, a year, or a lifetime? . . . They eyed each other with awful resignation.

The Hand of Emmagene

After high school she had come down from Hortons-
   burg
To find work in Nashville.
She stayed at our house.
And she began at once to take classes
In a secretarial school.
As a matter of fact, she wasn't *right* out of high school.
She had remained at home two years, I think it was,
To nurse her old grandmother
Who was dying of Bright's disease.
So she was not just some giddy young country girl
With her head full of nonsense
About running around to Nashville night spots
Or even about getting married
And who knew nothing about what it was to work.

From the very beginning we had in mind
—My wife and I did—
That she ought to know some boys
Her own age. That was one of our first thoughts.
She was a cousin of ours, you see—or of Nancy's.
And she was from Hortonsburg,
Which is the little country place
Thirty miles north of Nashville
Where Nancy and I grew up.

That's why we felt responsible
For her social life
As much as for her general welfare.
We always do what we can, of course,
For our kin when they come to town—
Especially when they're living under our roof.
But instead of trying to entertain Emmagene
At the Club
Or by having people in to meet her,
Nancy felt
We should first find out what the girl's interests were.
We would take our cue from that.

Well, what seemed to interest her most in the world
Was work. I've never seen anything quite like it.
In some ways, this seemed the oddest thing about her.
When she first arrived, she would be up at dawn,
Before her "Cousin Nan" or I had stirred,
Cleaning the house—we would smell floor wax
Before we opened our bedroom door some mornings—
Or doing little repair jobs
On the table linen or bed linen
Or on my shirts or even Nancy's underwear.
Often as not she would have finished
The polishing or cleaning she had taken upon herself to
    do
Before we came down. But she would be in the living
    room
Or sun parlor or den or dining room
Examining the objects of her exertions, admiring them,
Caressing them even—Nancy's glass collection
Or the Canton china on the sideboard.
One morning we found her with pencil and paper
Copying the little geometrical animals
From one of the oriental rugs.

Or some mornings she would be down in the kitchen
  cooking
Before the servants arrived
(And of course she'd have the dishes she'd dirtied
All washed and put away again before the cook
Came in to fix breakfast). What she was making
Down there in the pre-dawn hours
Would be a cake or a pie for Nancy and me.
(She didn't eat sweets, herself.)
Its aroma would reach us
Before we were out of bed or just as we started down the
  stairs.
But whether cleaning or cooking,
She was silent as a mouse those mornings.
We heard nothing. There were only the smells
Before we came down. And after we came down there'd
  be
Just the sense of her contentment.

    It was different at night. The washing machine
Would be going in the basement till the wee hours,
Or sometimes the vacuum cleaner
Would be running upstairs before we came up
Or running downstairs after we thought
We'd put the house to bed.
(We used to ask each other and even ask her
What she thought the cook and houseman
Were meant to do. Sometimes now we ask ourselves
What *did* they do during the time that Emmagene was
  here.)
And when she learned how much we liked to have fires
In the living room and den, she would lay them
In the morning, after cleaning out the old ashes.
But at night we'd hear her out in the back yard
Splitting a fireplace log, trying to get lightwood

Or wielding the ax to make kindling
Out of old crates or odd pieces of lumber.
More than once I saw her out there in the moonlight
Raising the ax high above her head
And coming down with perfect accuracy
Upon an up-ended log or a balanced two-by-four.

There would be those noises at night
And then we noticed sometimes the phone would ring.
One of us would answer it from bed,
And there would be no one there.
Or there would be a click
And then another click which we knew in all likelihood
Was on the downstairs extension.
One night I called her name into the phone—"Emma-
gene?"—
Before the second click came, just to see if she were there.
But Emmagene said nothing.
There simply came the second click.

There were other times, too, when the phone rang
And there would be dead silence when we answered.
"Who is it?" I would say. "Who are you calling?"
Or Nancy would say, "To whom do you wish to speak?"
Each of us, meanwhile, looking across the room at Em-
magene.
For we already had ideas then, about it. We had already
Noticed cars that crept by the house
When we three sat on the porch in the late spring.
A car would mosey by, going so slow we thought surely
it would stop.
But if Nancy or I stood up
And looked out over the shrubbery toward the street,
Suddenly there would be a burst of speed.

The driver would even turn on a cut-out as he roared
  away.

    More than once the phone rang while we were at the
    supper table
On Sunday night. Emmagene always prepared that meal
And did up the dishes afterward since the servants were
  off
On Sunday night. And ate with us too, of course.
I suppose it goes without saying
She always ate at the table with us.
She rather made a point of that from the start.
Though it never would have occurred to us
For it to be otherwise.
You see, up in Hortonsburg
Her family and my wife's had been kin, of course,
But quite different sorts of people really.
Her folks had belonged to a hard-bitten fundamentalist sect
And Nancy's tended to be Cumberland Presbyterians
Or Congregationalists or Methodists, at worst
(Or Episcopalians, I suppose I might say "at best").
The fact was, Nancy's family—like my own—
Went usually to the nearest church, whatever it was.
Whereas Emmagene's traveled thirteen miles each Sunday
  morning
To a church in the hilly north end of the County,
A church of a denomination that seemed always
To be *changing* its name by the addition of some qualify-
  ing adjective.
Either that or seceding from one synod or joining another.
Or deciding just to go it alone
Because of some disputed point of scripture.

    Religion aside, however, there were differences of style.
And Emmagene—very clearly—had resolved

Or been instructed before leaving home
To brook no condescension on our part.
"We're putting you in the guest room," Nancy said
Upon her arrival. And quick as a flash Emmagene added:
"And we'll take meals together?"
"Why of course, why of course," Nancy said,
Placing an arm about Emmagene's shoulder.
"You'll have the place of honored guest at our table."

   Well, on Sunday nights it was more like we
Were the honored guests,
With the servants off, of course,
And with Emmagene electing to prepare our favorite
Country dishes for us, and serving everything up
Out in the pantry, where we always take that meal.
It was as though we were all back home in Hortonsburg.
But if the phone rang,
Emmagene was up from the table in a split second
(It might have been her own house we were in)
And answered the call on the wall phone in the kitchen.
I can see her now, and hear her, too.
She would say "Hello," and then just stand there, listen-
     ing,
The receiver pressed to her ear, and saying nothing more
     at all.
At first, we didn't even ask her who it was.
We would only look at each other
And go back to our food—
As I've said, we were more like guests at her house
On Sunday night. And so we'd wait till later
To speak about it to each other.
We both supposed from the start
It was some boy friend of hers she was too timid to talk
     with
Before us. You see, we kept worrying

About her not having any boy friends
Or any girl friends, either.
We asked ourselves again and again
Who in our acquaintance we could introduce her to,
What nice Nashville boy we knew who would not mind
Her plainness or her obvious puritanical nature—
She didn't wear make-up, not even lipstick or powder,
And didn't do anything with her hair.
She wore dresses that were like maid's uniforms except
Without any white collars and cuffs.
Nancy and I got so we hesitated to take a drink
Or even smoke a cigarette
When she was present.
I soon began watching my language.

I don't know how many times we saw her
Answer the phone like that or heard the clickings
On the phone upstairs. At last I told Nancy
She ought to tell the girl she was free
To invite whatever friends she had to come to the house.
Nancy said she would have to wait for the opportunity;
You didn't just come out with suggestions like that
To Emmagene.

One Sunday night the phone rang in the kitchen.
Emmagene answered it, of course, and stood listening for
  a time.
Finally, very deliberately, as always,
She returned the little wall phone to its hook.
I felt her looking at us very directly
As she always did when she put down the phone.
This time Nancy didn't pretend
To be busy with her food.
"Who *was* that, Emmagene?" she asked
In a very polite, indifferent tone.

"Well, I'll tell you," the girl began
As though she had been waiting forever to be asked.
"It's some boy or other I knew up home.
Or *didn't* know." She made an ugly mouth and shrugged.
"That's who it always is," she added, "in case you *care* to
    know."
There was a too obvious irony
In the way she said "*care* to know."
As though we ought to have asked her long before this.
"That's who it is in the cars, too," she informed us—
Again, as though she had been waiting only too long for
    us to ask.
"When they're off work and have nothing better to do
They ring up or drive by
Just to make a nuisance of themselves."
"How many of them are there?" Nancy asked.
"There's quite some few of them," Emmagene said with
    emphasis.
"Well, Emmagene," I suddenly joined in.
"You ought to make your choice
And maybe ask one or two of them to come to the house
    to see you."
She looked at me with something like rage.
"They are not a good sort," she said. "They're a bad lot.
You wouldn't want them to set foot on your front steps.
Much less your front porch or in your house."

    I was glad it was all coming out in the open and said,
"They can't all be bad. A girl has to be selective."
She stood looking at me for a moment
In a kind of silence only she could keep.
Then she went into the kitchen and came back
Offering us second helpings from the pot of greens.
And before I could say more,

She had changed the subject and was talking about the
    sermon
She had heard that morning, quoting with evangelistic fer-
    vor,
Quoting the preacher and quoting the Bible.
It was as if she were herself hearing all over again
All she had heard that very morning
At that church of hers somewhere way over on the far
    side
Of East Nashville. It was while she was going on
About that sermon that I began to wonder for the first
    time
How long Emmagene was going to stay here with us.
I found myself reflecting:
She hasn't got a job yet and she hasn't got a beau.

    It wasn't that I hadn't welcomed Emmagene
        as much as Nancy
And hadn't really liked having her in the house.
We're always having relatives from the country
Stay with us this way. If we had children
It might be different. This big house wouldn't
Seem so empty then. (I often think we keep the servants
We have, at a time when so few people have any servants
    at all,
Just because the servants help fill the house.)
Sometimes it's the old folks from Hortonsburg we have
When they're taking treatments
At the hospital or at one of the clinics.
Or it may be a wife
Who has to leave some trifling husband for a while.
(Usually the couples in Hortonsburg go back together.)
More often than not it's one of the really close kin
Or a friend we were in school with or who was in our
    wedding.

We got Emmagene
Because Nancy heard she was all alone
Since her Grandma died
And because Emmagene's mother
Before *she* died
Had been a practical nurse and had looked after Nancy's
  mother
In her last days. It was that sort of thing.
And it was no more than that.
But we could see from the first how much she loved
Being here in this house and loved Nancy's nice things.
That's what they all love, of course.
That's what's so satisfying about having them here,
Seeing how they appreciate living for a while
In a house like ours. But I don't guess
Any of them ever liked it better than Emmagene
Or tried harder to please both Nancy and me
And the servants, too. Often we would notice her
Even after she had been here for months
Just wandering from room to room
Allowing her rather large but delicately made hands
To move lightly over every piece of furniture she passed.
One felt that in the houses she knew around Hortonsburg
—In her mother's and grandmother's houses—
There had not been pretty things—not things she loved to
  fondle.
It was heartbreaking to see her the day she broke
A pretty pink china vase that Nancy had set out in a new
  place
In the sun parlor. The girl hadn't seen it before.
She took it up in her strong right hand
To examine it. Something startled her—
A noise outside, I think. Maybe it was a car going by,
Maybe one of those boys. . . . Suddenly the vase crashed
  to the floor.

Emmagene looked down at the pieces, literally wringing
   her hands
As if she would wring them off, like chickens' necks if she
   could.
I was not there, Nancy told me about it later.
She said that though there was not a sign of a tear in the
   girl's eyes,
She had never before seen such a look of regret and guilt
In a human face. And what the girl said
Was even stranger. Nancy and I
Have mentioned it to each other many times since.
"I despise my hand for doing that," she wailed.
"I wish—I do wish I could punish it in some way.
I ought to see it don't do anything useful for a week."

    One night on the porch
When one of those boys went by in his car
At a snail's pace
And kept tapping lightly on his horn,
I said to Emmagene, "Why don't you stand up and wave
   to him,
Just for fun, just to see what happens? I don't imagine
They mean any harm."
"Oh, you don't know!" she said.
"They're a mean lot.
They're not like some nice Nashville boy
That you and Cousin Nan might know."
Nancy and I sat quiet after that,
As if some home truth had been served up to us.
It wasn't just that she didn't want to know
Those Hortonsburg boys.
She *wanted* to know Nashville boys
Of a kind we might introduce her to and approve of.
I began to see—and so did Nancy, the same moment—
That Emmagene had got ideas about herself

Which it wouldn't be possible for her to realize.
She not only liked our things. She liked our life.
She meant somehow to stay. And of course
It would never do. The differences were too deep.
That is to say, she had no notion of changing herself.
She was just as sure now
About what one did and didn't do
As she had been when she came.
She still dressed herself without any ornamentation
Or any taste at all. And would have called it a sin to do
    so.
Levity of any kind seemed an offense to her.
There was only one Book anyone need read.
Dancing and drinking and all that
Was beyond even thinking about.
And yet the kind of luxury we had in our house
Had touched her. She felt perfectly safe, perfectly good
With it. It was a bad situation
And we felt ourselves somewhat to blame.
Yet what else could we do
But help her try to find a life of her own?
That had been our good intention from the outset.

    I investigated those boys who did the ringing up
And the horn blowing. In Nashville you have ways
Of finding out who's in town from your home town.
It's about like being in Paris or Rome
And wanting to know who's there from the U.S.A.
You ask around among those who speak the home tongue.
And so I asked about those boys.
They were, I had to acknowledge, an untamed breed.
But, still, I said to Nancy, "Who's to tame 'em
If not someone like Emmagene? It's been going on
Up there in Horton County for, I'd say—well,
For a good many generations anyway."

The Hand of Emmagene

I don't know what got into us, Nancy and me.
We set about it more seriously, more in earnest,
Trying to get her to see something of those boys.
I'm not sure what got into us. Maybe it was seeing Emmagene
Working her fingers to the bone
—For no reason at all. There was no necessity.—
And loving everything about it so.
Heading out to secretarial school each morning,
Beating the pavements in search of a job all afternoon,
Then coming home here and setting jobs for herself
That kept her up half the night.
Suddenly our house seemed crowded with her in it.
Not just to us, but to the servants, too.
I heard the cook talking to her one night in the kitchen.
"You ought to see some young folks your own age.
You ought to have yourself a nice fellow."
"What nice young fellow would I know?" Emmagene
asked softly.
"I'm not sure there is such a fellow—not that I would know."
"Listen to her!" said the cook. "Do you think we don't see
Those fellows that go riding past here?"
"They're trash!" Emmagene said. "And not one of them
That knows what a decent girl is like!"
"Listen to her!" said the cook.
"I hear her," said the houseman, "and you hear her.
But she don't hear us. She don't hear nobody but herself."
"Ain't nobody good enough for you?" the cook said.
"I'd like to meet some boy
Who lives around here," the poor girl said.
And to this the cook said indignantly,
"Don't git above your raisin', honey."
Emmagene said no more. It was the most
Any of us would ever hear her say on that subject.
Presently she left the kitchen

And went up the back stairs to her room.

Yet during this time she seemed happier than ever
To be with us. She even took to singing
While she dusted and cleaned. We'd hear
Familiar old hymns above the washer and the vacuum
   cleaner.
And such suppers as we got on Sunday night!
Why, she came up with country ham and hot sausage
That was simply not to be had in stores where Nancy
   traded.
And then she *did* find a job!
She finished her secretarial training
And she came up with a job
Nowhere else but in the very building
Where my own office is.
There was nothing for it
But for me to take her to work in my car in the morning
And bring her home at night.

But there was a stranger coincidence than where her
   job was.
One of those boys from Hortonsburg turned out to run
   the elevator
In our building. Another of them brought up my car each
   night
In the parking garage. I hadn't noticed before
Who those young fellows were that always called me by
   name.
But then I noticed them speaking to her too
And calling her "Emmagene." I teased her about them a
   little
But not too much, I think. I knew to take it easy
And not spoil everything.

Then one night the boy in the garage
When he was opening the car door for Emmagene, said,
"George over there wants you to let him carry you home."
This George was still another boy from Hortonsburg
(Not one that worked in my building or in the garage)
And he saluted me across the ramp.
"Why don't you ride with him, Emmagene?" I said.
I said it rather urgently, I suppose.
Then without another word, before Emmagene could
    climb in beside me,
The garage boy had slammed my car door.
And I pulled off, down the ramp—
With my tires screeching.

At home, Nancy said I ought to have been ashamed.
But she only said it after an hour had passed
And Emmagene had not come in.
At last she did arrive, though
Just as we were finishing dinner.
We heard a car door slam outside.
We looked at each other and waited.
Finally Emmagene appeared in the dining-room doorway.
She looked at us questioningly,
First at Nancy's face, then mine.
When she saw how pleased we were
She came right on in to her place at the table
And she sat down, said her blessing,
And proceeded to eat her supper as though nothing un-
    usual had happened.

She never rode to or from work with me again.
There was always somebody out there
In the side driveway, blowing for her in the morning
And somebody letting her out in the driveway at night.
For some reason she always made them let her out

Near the back door, as though it would be wrong
For them to let her out at the front.
And then she would come on inside the house the back
way.

She went out evenings sometimes, too,
Though always in answer to a horn's blowing in the drive-
way
And never, it seemed, by appointment.
She would come to the living-room door
And say to us she was going out for a little ride.
When we answered with our smiling countenances
She would linger a moment, as if to be sure
About what she read in our eyes
Or perhaps to relish what she could so clearly read.
Then she would be off.
And she would be home again within an hour or two.

It actually seemed as if she were still happier with us
now
Than before. And yet something was different too.
We both noticed it. The hymn singing stopped.
And—almost incredible as it seemed to us—
She developed a clumsiness, began tripping over things
About the house, doing a little damage here and there
In the kitchen. The cook complained
That she'd all but ruined the meat grinder,
Dropping it twice when she was unfastening it from the
table.
She sharpened the wood ax on the knife sharpener—or
tried to—
And bent the thing so the houseman insisted
We'd have to have another.
What seemed more carelessness than clumsiness
Was that she accidentally threw away

One of Nancy's good spoons, which the cook retrieved
From the garbage can. Nancy got so she would glance at
    me
As if to ask, "What will it be next?—poor child."
We noticed how nervous she was at the table,
How she would drop her fork on her plate—
As if she intended to smash the Haviland—
Or spill something on a clean place mat.
Her hands would tremble, and she would look at us
As though she thought we were going to reprimand her,
Or as if she hoped we would.
One day when she broke off the head of a little figurine
While dusting, she came to Nancy with the head
In one hand and the body in the other.
Her two hands were held so tense,
Clasping so tightly the ceramic pieces,
That blue veins stood out where they were usually
All creamy whiteness. Nancy's heart went out to her.
She seized the two hands in her own
And commenced massaging them
As if they were a child's, in from the snow.
She told the girl that the broken shepherd
Didn't matter at all,
That there was nothing we owned
That mattered *that* much.

     Meanwhile, the girl continued to get calls at night
On the telephone. She would speak a few syllables
Into the telephone now. Usually we couldn't make out
    what she was saying
And we tried not to hear. All I ever managed
To hear her say—despite my wish not to hear—
Were things like "Hush, George," or "Don't say such
    things."
Finally one night Nancy heard her say:

"I haven't got the kind of dress to wear to such a thing."

That was all Nancy needed. She got it out of the girl
What the event was to be. And next morning
Nancy was downtown by the time the stores opened,
Buying Emmagene a sleeveless, backless evening gown.
It seemed for a time Nancy had wasted her money.
The girl said she wasn't going to go out anywhere
Dressed like that. "You don't think I'd put you in a dress
That wasn't proper to wear," said Nancy, giving it to her
    very straight.
"It isn't a matter of what you think
Is proper," Emmagene replied. "It's what he would think
    it meant—
George, and maybe some of the others, too."
They were in the guest room, where Emmagene was stay-
    ing,
And now Nancy sat down on the twin bed opposite
The one where Emmagene was sitting, and facing her.
"This boy George doesn't really misbehave with you,
Does he, Emmagene?" Nancy asked her. "Because if he
    does,
Then you mustn't, after all, go out with him—
With him or with the others."
"You know I wouldn't let him do that, Cousin Nan," she
    said.
"Not really. Not the real thing, Cousin Nan."
"What do you mean?" Nancy asked in genuine bewilder-
    ment.
The girl looked down at her hands, which were folded in
    her lap.
"I mean, it's my hands he likes," she said.
And she quickly put both her hands behind her, out of
    sight.

"It's what they all like if they can't have it any other
    way."
And then she looked at Nancy the way she had looked
At both of us when we finally asked her who it was on
    the telephone,
As though she'd only been waiting for such questions.
And then, as before, she gave more
Than she had been asked for.
"Right from the start, it was the most disgusting kind of
    things
They all said to me on the telephone. And the language,
    the words.
You wouldn't have known the meaning, Cousin Nan."
When she had said this the girl stood up
As if to tell Nancy it was time she leave her alone.
And with hardly another word Nancy came on to our
    room.
She was so stunned she was half the night
Putting it across to me just what the girl had told her
Or had tried to tell her.

      Naturally, we thought we'd hear no more about the
    dress.
But, no, it was the very next night, after dinner,
That she came down to us in the living room
And showed herself to us in that dress Nancy had bought.
It can't properly be said she was wearing it,
But she had it on her like a nightgown,
As if she didn't have anything on under it.
And her feet in a pair of black leather pumps—
No make-up, of course, her hair pulled back as usual into
    a knot.
There was something about her, though, as she stood there
With her clean scrubbed face and her freshly washed hair
And in that attire so strange and unfamiliar to her

That made one see the kind of beauty she had,
For the first time. And somehow one knew what she was
 going to say.
"I'll be going out," she said, searching our faces
As she had got so she was always doing when she spoke
 to us.
Nancy rose and threw her needlework on the chair arm
And didn't try to stop it when it fell onto the floor.
Clearly, she too had perceived suddenly a certain beauty
 about the girl.
She went over to her at once and said,
"Emmagene, don't go out with George again.
It isn't wise." They stepped into the hall
With Nancy's arm about the girl's waist.
"I've got to go," Emmagene said.
And as she spoke a horn sounded in the driveway.
"George is no worse than the rest," she said.
"He's *better*. I've come to like things about him now."
There was more tapping on the horn,
Not loud but insistent.
"He's not the kind of fellow I'd have liked to like.
But I can't stop now. And you've gone and bought this
 dress."

    Nancy didn't seem to hear her. "You mustn't go,"
she said.
"I couldn't live through this evening.
I'd never forgive myself." The horn kept it up outside,
And the girl drew herself away from Nancy.
Planting herself in the middle of the hall
She gave us the first line of preaching we'd ever heard from
 her:
"It is not for us to forgive ourselves. God forgives us."
Nancy turned and appealed to me. When I stood up
The girl said defiantly, "Oh, I'm going!"

She was speaking to both of us. "You can't stop me now!"
The car horn had begun a sort of rat-a-tat-tat.
"That's what he's like," she said, nodding her head
Toward the driveway where he was tapping the horn.
"You can't stop me now!
I'm free, white, and twenty-one.
That's what *he* says about me."
Still the horn kept on,
And there was nothing we could think to say or do.
Nancy did say, "Well, you'll have to have a wrap.
You can't go out like that in this weather."
She called to the cook, who came running
(She must have been waiting just beyond the hall door to
    the kitchen)
And Nancy sent her to the closet on the landing
To fetch her velvet evening cape.
There was such a commotion
With the girl running out through the kitchen,
The cape about her shoulders and billowing out behind,
Almost knocking over the brass umbrella stand,
I felt the best thing I could do was to sit down again.
Nancy and the cook were whispering to each other
In the hall. I could see their lips moving
And then suddenly I heard the groan or scream
That came from the kitchen and could be heard all over
    the house.

   I went out through the dining room and the pantry
But the cook got there first by way of the back hall door.
The cook said she heard the back door slam.
I didn't hear it. Nancy said afterward she heard
The car door slam. We all heard the car roar down the
    driveway
In reverse gear. We heard the tires whining
As the car backed into the street and swung around

Into forward motion. None of that matters,
But that's the kind of thing you tend to recall later.
What we saw in the kitchen was the blood everywhere.
And the ax lying in the middle of the linoleum floor
With the smeary trail of blood it left
When she sent it flying. The houseman
Came up from the servants' bathroom in the basement
Just when the cook and I got there.
He came in through the back porch.
He saw what we saw of course
Except he saw more. I followed his eyes
As he looked down into that trash can at the end of the
    counter
And just inside the porch door. But he turned away
And ran out onto the back porch without lifting his eyes
    again.
And I could hear him being sick out there.

    The cook and I looked at each other
To see who would go first.
I knew I had to do it, of course.
I said, "You keep Miss Nancy out of here,"
And saw her go back into the hall.
I went over to the trash can,
Stepping over the ax and with no thought in my head
But that I must look. When I did look,
My first thought was, "Why, that's a human hand."
I suppose it was ten seconds or so before I was enough
    myself
To own it was Emmagene's hand
She had cut off with the wood ax.
I did just what you would expect.
I ran out into the driveway, seeing the blood every step,
And then back inside, past the houseman still retching over
    the banister,

And telephoned the police on the kitchen telephone.
They were there in no time.

    The boy who had been waiting for Emmagene
In the car, and making the racket with his horn
Used better judgment than a lot of people might have.
When she drew back the velvet cape and showed him
What she had done to herself
And then passed out on the seat,
He didn't hesitate, didn't think of bringing her back inside
   the house,
He lit out for the emergency room at the hospital.
Though she was dead when he got her there,
It is probably true
That if anything at all could have saved her
It was his quiet thinking that would have done it.
Anyhow, everybody congratulated the boy—
The police, and the doctors as well.
The police arrested him in the emergency waiting room,
But I went down to the station that night
And we had him free by nine o'clock next morning.
He was just a big country boy, really,
Without any notion of what he was into.
We looked after arrangements for Emmagene, of course,
And took the body up to Hortonsburg for burial.
The pastor from her church came to the town cemetery
And held a graveside service for her.
He and everybody else said a lot of consoling things to us.
They were kind in a way that only country people
Of their sort can be,
Reminding us of how hospitable we'd always been
To our kinfolks from up there
And saying Emmagene had always been
A queer sort of a girl, even before she left home.
Even that boy George's parents were at the service.

Nancy and I did our best to make them see
George wasn't to be blamed too much.
After all, you could tell from looking at his parents
He hadn't had many advantages.
He was a country boy who grew up kind of wild no doubt.
He had come down to Nashville looking for a job
And didn't have any responsible relatives here
To put restraints upon him
Or to give him the kind of advice he needed.
That might have made all the difference for such a boy,
Though of course it wasn't something you could say
To George's parents—
Not there at Emmagene's funeral, anyway.

Daphne's Lover

WHEN MY FRIEND FRANK LACY AND I WERE thirteen and still wearing bell-bottomed sailor pants, he and I sat together one afternoon on the cement steps that led up to his family's house on Central Avenue. We were perched about midway on the wide flight, guarded on either side by a larger-than-life cement lion, couchant and cast in a rather more pebbly mixture than the steps were. Suddenly, in a voice that ranged up and down the scale, Frank burst out with "Ah, Vinton! Ah, Goodbar! Ah, Harbert!" These were the names of streets in the old-fashioned Annandale section of Memphis where my family lived, only a few blocks from the more fashionable Central Avenue section. "What noble old streets. What noble-sounding names!" said Frank. He was half joking, of course. Yet for Frank there was a mysterious aura about my neighborhood, as there was about any neighborhood that differed in the smallest degree from his own; as there was, I suppose, about any family whose routines and practices differed from those of his family.

When we were thirteen and younger it was mostly at Frank's house that he and I played together. When we got to be fourteen and fifteen—especially during those years—Frank spent a lot of time at my house. My parents and my three sisters became very fond of him during that period. It got so I was not surprised to come home from a movie on a Friday or Saturday night and find Frank sitting in the living room with my parents. They would be playing Canfield or Mah-Jongg or sometimes dominoes. Frank might be sitting at Dad's or Mother's elbow, watching the game closely. Or he might be lounging in an easy chair, in the far corner of the room, reading some magazine like *Collier's*. There was almost no magazine of general interest that didn't find its way into our house. On the other hand, magazines one saw at Frank's house usually appealed to some special interest, magazines like *Field and Stream* and *Vanity Fair*. Frank himself often bought magazines at the drugstore—new ones like *Esquire* and *Ballyhoo*. Instead of taking them home, he often as not brought them to our house to read and he would be up in my room reading an entire afternoon sometimes.

More than once I came home from an afternoon spent with other friends and found his magazines scattered on the floor of my room and Frank sprawled on my bed, taking a nap. If I found him with my parents, after a movie, he was apt to stay the night with us. My mother would always insist upon his telephoning home to let Mrs. Lacy know he wouldn't be coming in. Frank would say it wasn't necessary and would try to change the subject. If my three older sisters were present, he would enlist their aid in protesting the need for his calling. They always came to his support, too. They were charmed by Frank and would support him in any argument. But on this particular subject they were especially vociferous, because Frank made it so explicitly an issue of parental protectiveness. Smiling all the while and obviously admiring both my parents' firmness, he would accuse Mother of overprotecting her children and of setting up too many rules. My sisters would rally to his cause and urge him on.

"What would you do if your children disobeyed?" he would ask. But Mother could not be made to generalize.

She insisted upon her point. She never failed to make Frank telephone home. Yet I often suspected that when he went to the telephone out in the sun parlor and ostensibly made his call, Frank was actually holding down the receiver with his finger.

My mother's fondness for games was a matter of continuing interest to Frank. Moreover, that fondness of hers was our chief connection with the Lacys. She and Mrs. Lacy occasionally played bridge in the same foursome. But my mother much preferred playing cards at home with her family. The battle of the sexes was usually fought out across the card table at our house—and with considerable relish, too. In all games, either my father and I played against some combination of my sisters and my mother, or sometimes one of my uncles who lived nearby teamed up with me or my father. The rule was that members of the opposite sexes were never allowed to be partners in bridge or to play on the same side in any game, the only exception being made, for no very obvious reason, in the case of Frank.

Frank admired my father's enthusiasm for gardening. He used to come and work with him in our rose beds on spring and summer afternoons. One time when the rest of us were in the sun parlor working the *Liberty* puzzle together, Mother sent the Negro houseboy out with glasses of iced tea for Dad and Frank. The sight of them rising up from their manual labor to accept the attentions of the white-jacketed houseboy struck us as highly amusing. When finally they came inside, we laughed at them about it. My father merely shrugged and smiled at the absurd picture we painted of them. But Frank found the picture no less than wonderful. "Yes, it's wonderful!" he exclaimed, gesturing with both hands and then interlocking his fingers on the crown of his head as he leaned back in his chair. "It was a wonderful moment—just perfect! It is just precisely what you-all's life is like! I'll never forget it!"

It wasn't only *my* family that fascinated Frank, however. Like me, he was at times drawn to the families of our other friends. He was attracted to the Berrys and the McLeods and the Cravenses in much the same way that I was, except that with him the attraction would sometimes become obsessive. Joe Berry's family, for instance, was a family of invalids and hypochondriacs. The conversation at the Berrys' table was nearly always about illness and medicines, though never about death. Someone seemed always to be going into or coming out of the hospital. Joe Berry's parents, as well as his two grandfathers who lived in the house with them, seemed to have operation after operation without ever being critically ill. Joe had an imbecile sister Grace who was much in evidence at their house and was always spoken of as "the Baby." The Baby sometimes said dreadful things to one. For that reason most of us dreaded going to Joe's house. Through the screen door on the front porch she said to me once, "If I let you in, will you cut my throat and throw my head away?" I told Frank about this and he said she had said the same thing to him.

"What kind of answer can you give to something like that?" I asked.

"Oh, say anything," Frank advised, shrugging his shoulders.

"What did *you* say?" I asked.

"Me? Oh, I said, 'You bet your life I will if that's what you want.' "

He didn't mind the things Grace said. He would laugh at her indulgently with the rest of the family. He even got so he would talk their baby-talk to her. He would even take her for walks around the block, either with Grace leaning on his arm as they ambled slowly along or with him pushing her in her wheelchair.

Frank's intimacies with the Berrys ended with a misunderstanding of some sort. He and Joe continued to be friends, however, and later on the misunderstanding was forgotten. His intimacy with my family ended similarly. My father, during those Depression years, used often to threaten to move us back up to Jackson County, where he owned a lot of land as well as the old house he had grown up in, and where, as he said, "We could live on nothing a year." We never went back to Jackson County to live, of course, but as long as the Depression lasted it was the excuse for our making frequent weekend trips up there to buy produce at reduced rates from our tenant farmers. We would stay in my grandfather's old house for a day or so, then we would head for Memphis with the car laden with eggs, cured meat, and whatever fruits and vegetables were in season.

Returning from one of these expeditions one Sunday afternoon, we saw immediately that somebody had been occupying our house during our two days' absence. Papers and books were strewn carelessly about the living room. In the kitchen, unwashed dishes littered the table and sink. And yes, lo and behold, when I went up to my room he was "still there," stretched out on my bed asleep.

"It's Frank!" I called out from the top of the back stairs to the rest of the family. My Father was still bringing in produce from the car and packing it in the extra refrigerator he had installed in the back hall. I heard my mother say to him, "We should have known it was Frank. But how do you suppose he got in?" They treated Frank's being there quite casually. And Mother, who never bothered much about housekeeping, was not really disturbed by the disorder. But when word reached my three sisters, who were still out on the porch, that Frank had been in the house over the weekend, they came shrieking indoors, racing through the side hall and then up the stairs to their rooms.

"Oh, no! Oh, no!" they cried. The two younger girls roomed together, and from their room we presently heard them shouting, "Frank, how *could* you?" And from the oldest girl's room came groans and more "oh, no's." Only then did I remember the girls' diaries and how often they had mentioned them to Frank and how he had pleased them by saying he wished he could get hold of them sometime and read them. I looked at Frank. He stood there in the hallway with his eyes on the doors to the girls' rooms. The smile on his face was one of tolerance, not guilt. Finally he looked at me and said, "I didn't read a word of the stuff. But I found them in the most obvious places and I left them lying open on the tops of their bureaus. They would have been *too* disappointed if I hadn't."

Frank and I then went down the back stairs to the hall, where my mother and father were still putting away the produce. Frank offered to help them, but Mother smiled at him and suggested that, instead, he clear up some of the papers and books in the living room. Just then the telephone rang, and Frank said, "That thing rang all day yesterday."

"And you didn't answer it?" my father asked, pausing with his two hands in the refrigerator and looking over his shoulder at Frank.

"No, sir, I didn't," Frank said, meeting my father's gaze.

Mother answered the telephone there in the back hall. It was Frank's eldest brother, James. "Yes, I certainly do," we heard Mother say. "He's right here with us." But James didn't ask to speak to Frank, and, Mother remarked to us later, he did not seem greatly perturbed by Frank's having been out of touch with his family. He asked Mother to give Frank the message that Mrs. Lacy had been thrown from her horse while riding with a friend out at La Grange on Saturday morning, and that she was in the hospital and still unconscious.

I went with Frank immediately to the hospital, where we learned that within the past few minutes Mrs. Lacy had regained consciousness. Since she had suffered no injuries in the fall except for the assumed blow on her head, she was home from the hospital within a few days. The only permanent effect of the accident was that she could not recall any events of the twenty-four hours previous to it. And for this, it has been remarked by more than one person since, she might well be thankful, because Mrs. Lacy's companion on that early-morning ride at La Grange was a gentleman other than Frank's father.

This whole incident was very disturbing to my mother. Frank was never again on such familiar terms with her and my father. In the back hall, after she had told him of his mother's accident and while we were about to set out for the hospital, she could not resist asking, "Frank, *why* didn't you telephone and let them know where you were?" Frank shrugged. Though he was clearly concerned about his mother's condition, for one moment he seemed to give all his attention to my mother. He was observing how she responded to his having broken her rule. Although he never told me so, I was convinced from that moment that his holing up in our house was not done entirely for the purpose of pretending to read my sisters' diaries. Certainly he wished to please my sisters, but he wished also to learn what it would be like to break the rules that such a family as mine laid down.

As for Mother, it seemed incredible to her that the Lacy family was so little upset by not having known Frank's whereabouts during that weekend. In later years it was annoying to her that, whenever there was any reference made to the weekend, Mrs. Lacy could not—or would not—get it straight that Frank had been staying in our house all the while and had not gone up to Jackson County with us, as she obviously preferred to believe. The mess that Frank left in the kitchen and the disorder in the living room did not, as I have said, bother Mother. But his having failed to call home seemed unforgivable. Also, for days and days she and my father speculated upon how Frank could have got into the house. For some reason, I did not tell them the truth. Frank and I had, some weeks earlier, got duplicates made of our house keys and had exchanged them. I never made use of mine to his house, but for several years I continued to feel that there might be some circumstance when I would want to do so.

I WON'T TRY TO CONCEAL THE FACT THAT one of the things I have always admired most about Frank is his success with women. By the time he and I left home and went off to college, I had already participated vicariously in his countless romances. Even today his amorous involvements hold considerable fascination for me. They did so even when we were very small boys. Not that I didn't have girls of my own there in Memphis when he and I were growing up. I fell head over heels in love with a girl named Irene Kincaid long before there was even a soft down on my cheeks. By the time I was sixteen I had already met Mary Maxwell and knew then that she and I would someday be married. But if one has any imagination whatsoever, one has always to participate to some degree in the experience of one's friends. This is one conviction that Frank and I have always held in common. It may, indeed, be one that I have lived too much by. Nowadays, for instance, I take much too much interest in the activities of my grown-up children and even in the lives of my students at the University where I teach—even in the careers of my former students. I often reproach myself for interfering in my children's lives and for trying to direct the careers of my young friends. And I have to confess that out there in Memphis I had other contemporaries besides Frank Lacy whose lives were always just as interesting to me as Frank's and with whom I have kept in touch through all the years. It is almost as though I have lived the lives of these friends as well as my own life. The word for all this is *empathy*, of course, but that is the sort of educated word, cherished among my university colleagues, for which my old friends from Memphis have an aristocratic—or puritanical—distaste and which I shall, therefore, try to avoid using.

As children, Frank and I were plainly such different types that it was a matter of amusement to our mothers that we were friends at all. Our lives today—Frank off in Manhattan with his marriages and love affairs and his work always "in the vanguard of modern life," as he puts it, and I with my not unhappy domesticity in a remote university town, cultivating my garden, going off to Europe on an occasional foundation grant or attending a professional meeting somewhere—our lives today are not more different than our lives with our families were when we were boys. And the difference in our temperaments as adults is no more marked. Suffice it to say that I could not today sustain a series of love affairs any more easily than I could have tolerated, at twelve or fifteen, the little girls who always pursued Frank Lacy.

Behind the Lacys' great house on Central Avenue was an eight-foot wall which was no doubt built of some sort of cement blocks but was plastered over with the same stucco that covered the walls of the garage and of the Lacys' three-story, tile-roofed house itself. Beyond that wall and across an unpaved alley was a brick bungalow that faced upon the next street. I do not recall the name of the little girl who lived in that bungalow. Possibly I never knew it. (Possibly Frank Lacy himself never knew her name.) At the age of ten or so she wore her copper-red hair in a long

Dutch bob. Sometimes she would sit at the open dormer window on the rear of the bungalow and gaze out across the alley and over the stuccoed wall to where we were playing in Frank's back yard. She would sometimes, like any other little girl, be dressed up in one of her mother's evening dresses. And on every occasion her mouth would be rouged with heavy applications of lipstick. When she appeared there alone she pretended to pay no attention to us. She would only sit quietly, now and then moving languorously from one position on the window seat to another. But when one of her friends was with her there would be much giggling and darting to and from the window. The two little girls would throw kisses and call out, "I love you, Frank Lacy!" or "I love you, Alfred Lacy!" if Frank's brother happened to be present. One time the little redhead and her friend stood side by side at the window and in their squawky, birdlike voices serenaded us with verses from popular songs. But Frank would not ever— not even on that occasion—allow us to give any sign that we saw the girl at the dormer window. His parents had forbidden him, so he said, to take any notice of her. We knew better. We knew how little restraint the Lacy parents put upon him and his brothers, and knew that this restriction was of Frank's own making.

We came from school to play in the Lacys' yard one autumn afternoon. We arrived just in time to see the little redhead and her friend scurrying out through the gate in the stuccoed wall. And we saw right away what their business had been. On the wall was painted in red letters a foot high: "Red lips, kiss my blues away." And beneath that: "Some day I'll ride in your Packard, Frank Lacy." Almost before we could see the blushes on his cheeks, Frank had dashed into the garage, calling out to the Negro chauffeur, whom we could see through the open doors at work on one of the Lacys' cars. Frank returned presently with a brush and a bucket of buff-colored paint, and he began at once smearing the paint over the red lettering. While he was at work there, I noticed other areas of the wall that seemed to have been recently touched up with the same buff paint. For any other boy there would have ensued endless teasing. But we knew there could be no game that day if we began on Frank about the little redhead.

After a few minutes we were too engrossed in touch football to keep watch on the window beyond the wall. The other boys seemed to be too engrossed, at any rate. As for me, I could not resist glancing in that direction now and then. After a while I could hardly keep my eyes off the little redhead perched alone up there in the window, wearing a low-backed black bathing suit. I began to feel the impulse to throw something at her, the football or a big clod of dirt. Her exhibitionism offended and enraged me. This wasn't how a girl was supposed to behave toward boys! Or was it? All at once, in the midst of a play, I could endure it no longer. I withdrew from the play, cupped my hands to my mouth, and without at all understanding my impulse shouted the one word: "Whore!"

I don't know that the word had ever before passed my lips, or that I had a very clear notion of what it meant. Before the other boys fully comprehended what I had shouted even, Frank had leaped upon me, pushed me to the ground, and was pummeling me murderously. The cries of the other boys, as they tried to pull Frank off me, attracted the attention of the chauffeur. He came slowly to the garage entrance and called out, "Frank, you better get inside, you had, and get to your homework."

They had pulled Frank to his feet now. He hardly seemed to know who it was he had been fighting. "What made anybody say that?" he asked of the group. Then he glanced at the Negro man in the garage doorway and said simply, "All right, Glenway." It seemed a strange response. We all knew well enough that Frank and his brothers were not required to give any obedience to family servants. Frank pretended to comply, but of course it was really his own decision. Giving us a threatening look, as if to say he wanted no talk about the matter after he was gone, he walked away and in through the back door. The game broke up almost immediately.

The football we had been using was mine, and as soon as Frank was inside the house, I picked it up and set out alone across the wide boulevard that was Central Avenue, over the streetcar tracks that still ran on Central in those days, and on toward my own neighborhood—past Goodbar, past Harbert, past Vinton—on toward my family's house on Peabody. I suppose I purposely did not wait to walk with the other boys. I wanted to think about how Frank had behaved. I couldn't understand it. I still wanted to make that little redhead change her ways. And that was what Frank didn't seem to understand or like about me. With such thoughts in my head, the prosaic small-talk of those other boys would have seemed too intolerably boring.

A FEW DOORS TO THE WEST OF THE LACYS' house, on the opposite side of the street, there lived a girl named Janet Turner. Janet and Frank were taken for walks together by their nurses when they were infants. They later attended the same kindergarten. Even as a toddler, Janet was a rough child. She teased Frank and quarreled and fought with him so continually that when finally they were too old to have their nurses and parents choose their friends, Frank would have no more to do with her. That is, for a number of years he would not.

Janet became famous among the children of our generation as a tomboy. Since those were the Depression years, most people, even the Lacys, spent their summers at home in Memphis and somehow managed to endure the heat. The result for us children was that we, more than those who came just before or just after us, grew up spending our summers mostly at the Country Club. Janet Turner, at the Country Club, was nothing less than a holy terror. She would outplay most of us boys in the golf and tennis tournaments and lord it over us mercilessly. At the swimming pool she was eternally pushing somebody—usually a boy—into the water or spraying or ducking some boy whom she didn't even know. Yet by the time she and Frank were in their early teens, Frank had developed a tolerance for her beyond what most of us felt. His tolerance toward Janet was difficult for me to fathom, especially since she was among the few people toward whom I had ever seen him show contempt. When he and I were in the third grade at Miss Pentecost's School we walked past Janet Turner's house one winter day in the snow. Janet was at the top of the steep driveway that went up to her house; she was about to descend on a sled. When she saw us she stood up and recited the following rhyme for our benefit:

"Young lads and old gentlemen, take my advice:
Pull down your pants and slide on the ice."

Then throwing herself on the sled, she came tearing down the icy driveway. As she went past us and out into the street, Frank turned his back and said, "Ugh." She looked up at us as she went by and seemed delighted by the noise Frank had made. The sled carried her on out into the street, where the driver of an automobile slammed on his brakes and narrowly missed hitting her. But Janet got up from her sled clearly pleased by the narrowness of her escape, brushed herself off, and smiled hatefully at the driver.

"You might have got killed," I took it upon myself to say to her.

"It would have served her right," said Frank, with his nose in the air. I thought he looked a little pale, though.

It is the only thing of the sort I have ever heard Frank Lacy say to any girl or woman. And Janet ran up the driveway, pulling her sled behind her and grinning from ear to ear. "You might have got killed," I called after her. "I wish you had."

Without looking at me Frank said, "That's the sort of thing she likes to make you say."

But by the time we were in high school Frank seemed to have forgotten his dislike for that girl. Even before high school there had been periods when one would see them sitting together on her front steps—or his—sometimes at twilight of a weekday, sometimes on a Saturday morning. They became good friends. No more than that, however—not in Frank's mind. I remember "breaking in" on them once when they were dancing together at a sorority formal given at the Nineteenth Century Club. We were in high school then, and Frank and I each had a girl we went out with regularly. Frank's girl all through high school was Mary Edenton. Like my girl, also named Mary—Mary Maxwell—Frank's Mary Edenton attended Miss Hutchison's School, was a member of SKS sorority, and was the daughter of parents who belonged to the Memphis Country Club. But at dances Frank was always punctilious about dancing with all girls in our acquaintance, even the most unattractive ones. Janet Turner was by no means unattractive, despite her tomboyishness. Yet timid boys like me were often nervous about what she might say or do in public. Alone with a boy she was a model of propriety, but in public she was difficult. She danced cheek-to-cheek, required her partner to hold her very close, and she often danced without her shoes—a thing which in those days was considered altogether outlandish by chaperons. Moreover, when she was broken in on while dancing with a partner whom she had not enjoyed, she might say to him, "So long, Fumble Foot." Or if she had enjoyed the dance, she was apt to kiss her partner tenderly on the lips while her new partner looked on.

When I broke in on her and Frank at the Nineteenth Century Club, she held on to Frank's hand for a moment and said to him, "Frank, you're such a divine dancer and you're so chivalrous, too—yes, so god-damned, self-righteously chivalrous." Then she let go of his hand. He stood a moment smiling at Janet and even blew her a kiss. When she and I had danced away from him over the Nineteenth Century Club's parquet, she said in my ear, "Did you see that smile on his face? It was his forgiving smile. He *forgave* me because I am a *mere girl*."

Janet was an exceptionally good dancer, and I liked dancing with her even if she did talk to me about Frank. I knew already that I was going to marry my girl Mary Maxwell and knew—or so it seems to me now—that we would raise our four fine children and at the age of forty-five find as much satisfaction in each other's company as we did at fifteen. But Janet Turner did not seem to me a girl that anyone could ever make a life with; I couldn't imagine anyone ever marrying her.

When Janet finished at Bennington College, just before the outbreak of World War II, she became an airplane stewardess. It was considered the adventurous and rather fashionable thing for a girl like Janet to do in those days. But Janet was killed when the airliner she was aboard crashed near Newark in 1942. Frank had not seen her for two or three years before she was killed, but at the time he wrote me a letter blaming her father—that is, along with her three older brothers. When I received Frank's letter at Fort Oglethorpe, where I was stationed during the first two years of the war, it for some reason brought back to me still another incident that had occurred during the time we were in high school—the summer after our junior year.

We had been watching the Sunday-night movie in the main lounge at the Country Club. When the movie was over, a group of us wandered out onto the wide veranda that used to go round three sides of the old clubhouse. (The old clubhouse was a pleasant, unpretentious building, not at all like the trite Georgian place they have put up since the War.) Frank was there with Mary Edenton. Janet Turner and two other girls were there without escorts. We were on the part of the veranda that overlooked the swimming pool. Frank and Mary had strolled to the edge of the porch and stood by the banister looking out over the dark water of the pool. On his long left forefinger Frank was absent-mindedly twirling his key ring. Without anyone's noticing what she was about, Janet Turner sidled up to Frank. Suddenly she snatched the ring of keys from his finger and flung them out over the terrace directly below us and into the pool. Since the terrace lights had already been put out for the night, no one could see precisely where the keys fell into the water. We only saw them flying through the air, for one moment reflecting the light from the clubhouse windows, and then heard the little splash they made. When the keys hit the water, a gasp went up from the group assembled on the porch. And then there followed an outburst of laughter and shouting. But Frank's Mary Edenton, a beautiful, soft-spoken girl, bent forward a little over the banister railing and looked past Frank toward Janet. "Why in the world did you do that, Janet?" she asked. "What a silly thing it was to do." And my own date, Mary Maxwell, who was standing beside me on the shadowy porch and leaning on my arm, said, "How childish, Janet! How *very* childish! Why can't you grow up?"

Frank was leaning far out over the railing, trying vainly

to determine what part of the pool the keys had fallen into. He seemed to pay no attention to the laughter and heckling that came from the other boys, but when the girls began to berate Janet, he turned around to them and said, "What's the matter with you girls? Can't you take a joke?" Then, looking at Janet and smiling at her, he made a broad gesture with his hand and proclaimed to the whole porch, "Besides, you can't in justice blame Janet! Poor girl is not responsible." Everybody laughed. But Frank suddenly put on a serious expression. He had said something he had not meant to say. Presently he was striding along the veranda toward the steps that went down to the terrace, and from the terrace he disappeared into the basement locker rooms. Inside, he got someone to turn on the terrace lights.

He soon reappeared, wearing his swimming trunks. A cheer went up from the little crowd that now lined the railing. At that age particularly, Frank looked better than anyone else among us in swimming trunks. He was long-legged, with wide, rather sloping shoulders, and though he was barely seventeen his chest and arm muscles were already fully developed. He loped along the edge of the pool, landing lightly on the balls of his feet, and then about midway he turned quickly and made a shallow dive, a dive so neat that its splash sounded hardly greater than that the key ring had made. He was a first-rate swimmer and diver, and one might have suspected he welcomed this exhibition before his friends except for the modesty and understatement of that quick turn and almost silent entry into the water. He moved from the terrace into the water without full realization that he had exchanged elements. Swimming underwater, he swept along near the tile floor of the pool with nearly the same cadence that one had felt in his loping along the pool's edge. As we watched him in the water under the bright lights, we heard Janet Turner say with heavy irony to Mary Edenton, "Isn't he elegant, Mary?

Doesn't he do everything wonderfully? You two make a beautiful pair. I think you two were just made for each other." Most of us, I suppose, were embarrassed *for* Janet, and we expressed our embarrassment with our silence. As a matter of fact, Mary Edenton was the only one at this point who seemed no longer annoyed or embarrassed by Janet. "Aren't you silly?" she said indulgently to Janet.

Mary was a girl of great personal dignity, and her composure at that moment was quite in character. She was a tall girl with chestnut hair that she wore parted in the center and with a bun low on her rather long neck. (It is still impossible for me to look at a Raphael Madonna without thinking of her.) Her coiffure was flattering to her long, straight nose and pretty little chin; and it made her look somewhat older than other girls of seventeen. Moreover, Mary Edenton's long, handsome legs and her decidedly mature figure did not fail to catch the eye of many an older boy—boys whose attentions to her were resented by all the boys our age. But it *is* true that she and Frank made a "beautiful pair." I know from what my wife Mary has told me in recent years that Mary Edenton believed then, beyond all doubt, that she and Frank were going to have a long, happy married life together in Memphis. It was because she so identified herself with Frank, of course, that she could manage to take his view of Janet. She told other girls that Frank regarded Janet as a sort of bad little sister—which he had never had and perhaps missed having. Mary Edenton cheered and applauded Frank with the rest of us that night on the Country Club veranda. But by the time Frank was out of the pool and went hurrying toward the locker room below us, Janet Turner and her two friends had already slipped away from the scene.

When Frank had said Janet was "not responsible," I suspect that he meant only to be joshing her and that suddenly he recalled having heard his elders assert that very thing about her in all seriousness. He was afraid she might take him seriously and might think he wished to be cruel to her, because what Frank's parents would have meant by saying Janet was not responsible for her behavior was that her mother had died when she was an infant and that she had been brought up by her widowed father and her three older brothers—with the help, of course, of servants. She had no older sister nor mother to model herself upon or to be instructed by. Her brothers were the same ages as Frank's older brothers and were their cronies. Perhaps it was natural that Janet should think Frank and she ought to be friends. Perhaps her confusion was deeper than that, even. It was a matter Frank used to speculate upon, though only in the kindest way. . . . I listened to Frank's speculations in those days without making any of my own. But in recent years I commented to him once that I thought nothing might have changed his life—especially his relations with women—so much as would his possibly having had one of my older sisters for *his* sister instead of having had those three brothers of his. The suggestion clearly offended him. (That's how it often is with an old friend you have not been as close to recently as in the old days. You don't know what things may have happened to him to make him sensitive in new areas.) He replied by declaring with a good deal of feeling that if that were true, it might also be true that if I had had one of his brothers for a brother instead of having had only my three sisters, it might equally have affected my view of women. He suggested that I might not have taken women "so for granted," by which he meant, I suppose, that I don't find them as disturbing or as exciting as he does.

The Turners' house was only a few doors to the west of the Lacys', but it was on the opposite side of the broad boulevard with its streetcar tracks in a gravel roadbed down the center. When Janet was fourteen, her three brothers owned together a yellow Chevrolet roadster trimmed in black. During the winter the brothers were away in prep school and college. (Janet would be sent off to Chatham Hall the following year.) Janet taught herself to drive the roadster, just as Frank Lacy and I did with our family cars, by running it in and out of the garage, turning it around in the paved area behind the house, backing down the driveway and racing it up the driveway and into the garage. Of course there were times when all of us went farther abroad than that, accompanied by a father, a big brother, or a family chauffeur. But Janet eventually took advantage of her freedom at home and would be seen cruising up and down Central Avenue with the top to the roadster put back and with her English bulldog riding in the seat beside her. This was of course three years before the episode of the key ring and the Country Club pool, and with her head of tight, dark curls—she always wore her hair cut short—Janet looked like a really small child behind the wheel of the car. She presented a spectacle which all the neighborhood found disquieting but which nobody took any steps to interfere with.

Yet perhaps her performance failed after all to attract the eye of the only neighbor whose attention she cared for, because soon she was inspired to something far more spectacular. On a Sunday morning or in the middle of a weekday afternoon, when there was little or no traffic on Central Avenue, Frank Lacy would receive a telephone call from Janet. She would say, "Watch for us, Frank! And save us, Frank! We're on our way!" Then she would hang up the phone. Within three or four minutes Frank would see the Chevrolet, with its top back and nobody behind the steering wheel, with Janet and the bulldog sitting very erect in the rumble seat, passing slowly down the other side of Central Avenue. The girl had somehow learned to fix the accelerator, to lock the steering wheel, and to set the car on a westward course down the avenue. No matter how Frank was occupied he would run from the house and out into the street and on across the streetcar tracks to jump into the front seat and seize the wheel of the car. He would drive Janet home without speaking a word to her and would deliver the keys to the maid at the back door. But as they rode along, Janet Turner, throwing her head of curls from side to side, would be hugging the big, ugly bulldog and crooning, "Oh, he saved us, Clemson. Our hero saved us, Clemson. How can we ever thank him?"

IRENE KINCAID WAS A BLUE-EYED BLONDE with a profile like that of a girl on a Greek vase. From the time I was eleven until at fifteen I met the girl I was to marry, the very thought of Irene Kincaid's face and figure could literally make my heart pound underneath my shirt. So far as coloring is concerned, I have never to this day seen her fair complexion and blue eyes and pale gold hair surpassed. My love for her was quite pathetic, because she and I never had a taste or interest in common, and most certainly she never showed a flicker of romantic interest in me. She pretended to care for me, but I never had any real illusion. While I was eleven, twelve, and thirteen I was wholeheartedly in love with her and I permitted her to pretend she regarded me as her sweetheart and sometimes permitted her to treat me as a slave. Even until I was fifteen I was at least halfheartedly in love with Irene, though during the last year or so I scarcely ever saw her.

The case was this: I became enamored of Irene Kincaid without our having exchanged two words and without my having any notion of what sort of person she was. In appearance she was that very ideal of feminine beauty which had formed in my mind before I ever saw her. How such a particularized idea comes into being for a boy is a mystery. It comes from within, is dictated by one's own nature.

But no more than that can be said. How and when it becomes recognizable to the boy himself, how and when he becomes fully conscious of it, is another matter. I am sure I first recognized my own ideal among some rather stiff drawings that illustrated a book on Greek mythology, a book I found in the library in the fifth grade at Miss Pentecost's School. There was a drawing of a scantily clad Daphne being pursued by a togaed Apollo, both with thong-laced legs. The limbs of the Daphne in that drawing—still in their human form—were presented by the artist with a certain delicate subtlety which gave both a stout and a fragile effect—stout enough, that is, to let her run a good race but so fragile somehow that one didn't doubt they would change their form under the rude hands of the pursuing Apollo. I have seen many other graphic representations of that myth, but none has ever pleased me so well. The head of that artist's Daphne was no doubt copied directly from the head of some piece of fifth-century Greek sculpture, and its effect upon me would last my lifetime. I have in my study nowadays, set on the mantelpiece across from my writing desk, a Limoges figurine of Daphne and Apollo. It is often the first object that catches my eye when I look up from my work at the end of an evening, and somehow the sight of it is curiously relaxing to me. Or if my eye lights on it when I have first come down in the morning and am stuffing my papers into my briefcase before going over to the University, the little doll Daphne on my mantel never fails to lift my spirits. Ten years ago, supported by a foundation grant, my wife Mary and I spent a winter in Rome. We had a choice of three or four apartments, and I chose the one nearest to the Borghese Gardens. I forget now what the real reason for my preference was, but afterward I liked to say it was the proximity to the Bernini Daphne and Apollo in the Borghese Gallery. Mary would laugh at me and say, "I thought it was Greek sculpture you like so well. Bernini is a far cry from the Greeks."

And I would reply, "You don't understand. I like anybody's Daphne. In my mind I always translate her into Greek."

Another year, when Mary had inherited a little sum from an aunt in Memphis, we rented a villa for the summer on the French Riviera—at Cap-Martin. We took the house sight unseen, having got it from a listing in the London *Times*—on the rack in the university library. To our real consternation, on taking possession of the place, we found that one wall of the upstairs sitting room was decorated with nothing other than a fresco of Daphne and Apollo. It had been executed rather crudely, to say the least, by the hand of the English lady who owned the villa. Apollo was pictured in the brown garb of an English hunter—hat, boots, cartridge belt, and all. He was in hot pursuit of a stark-naked Daphne at whose knees and elbows and on whose backsides were sprouting what looked like fern fronds. After a moment of speechlessness, my wife exclaimed, "Translate *that* if you can!" I spent several days trying not to see the picture. But since it was the custom of the maid, who came with the house, to serve breakfast in that upstairs room, it was impossible to avoid it. The shocking thing, though, is that within a matter of a week or so I *was* able to work out some degree of translation in my mind. I found something beautiful in it. In the features of that Daphne's face—though certainly not in the features of her spindly English frame—there was the very vaguest suggestion that that English lady, too, had been stirred by the Greek conception of feminine beauty when she was a child. My wife could never see this in the picture. But it was there. Perhaps for me it is there in any artist's Daphne. In time, I came to like being in the room with that monstrous fresco. And when recently we have talked of going to France again, I have found myself wondering if the villa at Cap-Martin mightn't be available next summer.

At any rate, let me say that Irene Kincaid was beautiful in my eyes. I do not know that she was so in Frank Lacy's eyes, however, and there was never any way for me to know. Because from the afternoon I introduced him to her, the very mention of her name in my presence seemed a matter of embarrassment to him.

I am certain that until the present day Frank considers that he took Irene away from me. In a sense, he did. Yet in the most real sense she was never mine. At that age I would not have presumed to touch any girl, especially not the one I was in love with. It would have been unthinkable. I could not have loved her afterward, I was sure. My touch, it seemed to me, would surely turn her into some vegetable or leafy shrub about which I would have no feeling. Yet Irene, at the age of twelve, longed to receive the attention of boys, to go out on dates with them, to be made love to. She accepted the childish presents I gave her and allowed me to buy her a milkshake at the drugstore on Saturdays. But she treated me with the condescension of my older sisters. I don't know what would have happened if she had taken me seriously, don't know what I might have done or how it might have changed my whole life. But anyhow she thought I was "cute" and "funny" and rather a "goody-good." One day we were standing in front of a neighborhood movie theater and she began giggling at the sight of a couple kissing in a picture on the billboard. I turned my back on her and walked away down the sidewalk. But she ran and caught up with me at once and assured me that it was something else that had made her giggle. With me she always tried to be a perfect little lady. Yet in her flirtations with other boys at the drugstore I saw her behave quite differently. I have no doubt, though, that she turned out well as a woman. Years later I heard she had married an Englishman and was living in London. I have never run into her over there, but I suspect she is living quietly in one of the London suburbs and that she is a faithful, loving wife and mother. Such girls often turn out so, I believe.

On weekday afternoons Irene and I frequently played fly-ball together in her back yard. One afternoon I brought Frank home from school with me. We walked around the corner to Irene's house on Vinton Avenue. She was coming in from school. Since her family were Roman Catholics, she attended a Catholic girls' school at Crosstown. She came along Vinton that afternoon dressed in the navy-blue jumper that was her school's uniform, carrying an armload of books. When she saw us she smiled and, in trying to free her hand to wave, almost dropped her books. Frank and I began running toward her. I reached out my arms to take the books, and she held them out toward me at first, though her eyes were on Frank. Then she withdrew the books from me and offered them to Frank, saying archly, "You take them, whoever you are." Frank accepted the books, but carried them only a few steps before handing them over to me. "Oh, you lazybones!" cried Irene. Suddenly slipping her arm through his she said, "You'll be sorry you didn't carry my books. You'll have to carry me, instead." And she put all her weight on his arm.

Her mother met us at the door and invited us to go back to the big, bright breakfast room in the rear of the house and have a snack with Irene. A plate of pralines was on the table, and Irene brought out three glasses and filled two of them with milk, one for herself and one for me. Looking at Frank, she said, "Oh, I forgot about you." I remember feeling there was something common about the very sing-song way she said it. Then she filled his glass less than halfway up. He looked at her, pretending to frown. She said, "Say please." It was just the way I had seen her

behave with older boys at the drugstore. I wished I had
not brought Frank along. For the first time in my life I felt
the impulse to bash a girl with my fist. Presently Frank
said, "Please," smiling at her with his eyes closed. It was
as if he had withdrawn momentarily to analyze the situation. When he opened his eyes, he wore an astonished
expression. It was as if he were seeing her for the first time.
He reached out and seized the bottle of milk and filled his
glass. "I am the master of my fate," he said, suddenly
beating his breast. Irene laughed breathlessly. I only sighed
and shook my head, reflecting how mistaken Frank was in
what he had said.

Later, in Irene's back yard, the three of us played fly-
ball. But when we first went outside Irene threw me the
ball and called, "Keep-away!" Frank dashed at me, and I
returned the ball to Irene. He was much too tall and too
quick for her to be able to throw the ball back to me. She
turned and ran toward a clump of shrubbery. From there
on out it was mostly a game of chase, or hide-and-seek,
between the two of them. Now and then Frank would look
at me and shrug his shoulders, as if to say, What can I do
but give chase if that's what she wants? . . . I was thoroughly disgusted by Irene's behavior. Yet that little girl
seemed to have forgotten how I liked her to behave. She
would not let me catch her eye, but whenever she got an
opening she threw the ball to me, and I returned it. Finally,
though, I took up the bat and managed to get the fly-ball
game going. It went along all right until Irene's turn at bat
came. She hit the ball up into the branches of a tree, and
it came down on the other side of the tree trunk. She ran
to base and headed back toward home plate. Frank retrieved the ball and threw it to me. Irene was caught between us. We closed in on her, but Frank carefully threw
above her head. At last, at a moment when I had the ball,
she turned toward Frank and ran fullforce into him. As

they met, a shout or a scream or a shriek—*some* kind of noise—came out of my throat, but I believe neither of them heard it. I stood watching them with my mouth hanging open. It seemed the most natural thing in the world the way he then took her in his arms, bending her backward over his right arm, with his right foot set forward a little, and kissed her directly on the lips. It seemed to me that they held the kiss for several minutes. Her left arm moved gently about his neck, and I won't ever forget how her free right arm fell loosely behind her as she bent backward and how relaxed and beautiful and almost marble-like the arm seemed to me.

Strange to say, the game of fly-ball was taken up again immediately—and with none of us making any reference to the embrace. Perhaps we were all three absorbed in our private reflections. My feeling toward Frank was merely one of annoyance. It was so like him to want to give her what she required of him. In a sense what he had done was more servile than was my own book-toting sort of slavery. I went on thinking of Irene Kincaid as my girl for a long time after that day—for a year or so, that is. I would sometimes imagine myself taking her in my arms and kissing her, but I never did—never tried to, even. Frank, I discovered, soon began going to see her alone. He would never talk to me about her, but he would say simply that he had seen her. She may have been the first girl he ever kissed. She may even—a year or so later, I would imagine—have been the first girl he ever took to bed. He continued to have dates with her occasionally for as long as four or five years after that day, well into the time when I had already met Mary Maxwell and had set my mind firmly on the notion that I would someday marry her. Irene didn't go to any of the schools that most of the girls we knew did. Frank and I got so we didn't often see her. I suspect that when Frank saw her it was usually after he had quarreled with some other girl he was going with.

The little redhead who had lived behind the Lacy's house moved away from Memphis when her father took a job somewhere else. (She wrote a beautiful farewell letter to Frank, promising that they would meet later on in life.) But Irene merely moved out into another circle. She continued to live on Vinton Avenue but she was, from that time on, just as definitely and permanently lost from our view as the little redhead. Frank and I met other girls; we were at an age when the world began to seem sometimes full of nothing but girls. And though Frank's acquaintance among them was wider than mine, and his relationships with them always more intimate, still, in my mind at least, even I had a number of girls. Once I had met Mary Maxwell, of course, that was all over with for me. But from the time of my meeting with Mary my interest in Frank's romances seemed greater than ever, somehow. It was as if once I knew what my own life was to be, I needed to participate more wholeheartedly in the lives of others. It was as if I could only sustain my own kind of life and find satisfaction in it by allowing myself that participation. I tell myself nowadays—whenever I find myself thinking too much about my friends, my children, or my students, wondering about the details of their lives, their love life, their sex life—I tell myself that a healthy imagination is like a healthy appetite and must be fed. If you do not feed it the lives of your friends, I maintain, then you are apt to feed it your own life, to live in your imagination rather than upon it.

Her Need

    Her girlhood gone
Her husband in the suburbs with his second wife
She drives her teen-age son to his summer job
Each morning at six.
Wearing the horn-rimmed glasses required
By her license, and watching with nervous glances
At all intersections,
She goes fifty miles an hour and more
Through the congested streets of the old part of town
Where she and the boy live.
    Her driving is all that's reckless
Left in her life. Her son remarks this coolly
To himself, lounging beside her in the front seat,
And even about her reckless driving, the boy observes,
A certain nervous care is taken—
Even if only at the intersections.
He thinks, "Next year I'll learn to drive the car myself"
    She has her own job
In the neighborhood bank (assistant to the manager).
She is so efficient in her work there
They've tried twelve times to promote her
To the downtown office.
But she says, "No,
I'll do my time here at midtown

Where I know my way round, where I once lived with
    my parents,
Where I sowed a few wild oats, too few perhaps
—Oh, the things we didn't dare do that they all do now!—
Where I was married and had my baby
And thought myself happy for a time,
Actually thought I was satisfied with life.
No, I'll do better, as a woman,
Just to serve out my time here at midtown
Until retirement."
    "But you're young still, by banking standards,"
The bank manager tells her.
"Moreover, we *want* women
In banking nowadays.
A *man* your age
Would not have been advanced half so fast as you've been,
Even though he'd started out, as I did,
At a much younger age than you, my dear."
    The people downtown have several times called her in
And urged her to come downtown
And work in the main office for a while.
Then she would inevitably go out somewhere
As a branch manager herself!
"Where?" she says, suspiciously.
She must always ask that question.
She can't somehow stop herself.
"To which branch?"
She tries to imagine herself
In one of those other parts of town
That she never went into as a girl.
And she doesn't feel like herself at all.
She feels like something
That somebody else has made up,
Not something she herself became.
"To which branch?" she asks.

But they can't answer that.
They can't say for sure.
That's not the way they operate.
And she knows in her heart she doesn't want them to.
She sits there in the downtown office
Shaking her head.
    "See here," says the bank president finally,
"We're thinking of your own good.
We want to do our best by you.
We want you to rise in our organization."
But she can't understand why they are so ambitious
For her. The president is a man
Old enough almost to be her father
(He's told her again and again
How he knew and admired her father).
Wearing horn-rimmed spectacles like her own
He leans across his desk toward her.
He takes off his spectacles and shakes them at her
As he speaks,
And wipes the lenses and wipes his eyes,
Neither of which need wiping.
But he is very convincing
—Very like her father.
"What I'm trying to say to you, young lady"
(He doesn't dream how much she loathes
Being called young lady. She's *not* young.
Ask her son. Ask her former husband.)
"What I'm trying to say
Is that we value you. To put it plainly,
We think you're a whizz!"
    And suddenly she blurts out,
"But why didn't you tell me twenty years ago I was a
    whizz?"
    The banker, genuinely baffled, says,
"I didn't know you twenty years ago, my dear."

She lets it go at that.
For how could he have known her?
She didn't know herself then.
In those days, no smart girl knew herself.
She never guessed in those days
—Nobody like her father
Had ever given her a clue—
She had never guessed
While sowing her few wild oats and getting married
That she was a whizz
Or might become a whizz.
Why hadn't she ever had an inkling of it?
Why had nobody like her father
Ever given her a clue.
And, to make it worse,
Why must someone tell her now
When it was twenty years too late.

    It didn't matter, though.
It really didn't. Not to her.
Not driving her son to his summer job at six a.m.
Only at nine it matters a little.
At nine
She walks to the bank—the midtown branch—
Without her driving glasses and better groomed
Than at six.
She looks the way she's supposed to look
—Not too feminine,
Not too masculine.
Neither man nor woman
Could find cause to be jealous of her.
She looks perfect for her job.
But she thinks to herself:
"It wasn't always so,"

Thinks it without regret or rancor,
Thinks it, rather, as she does all things nowadays
In order to set the record straight,
To keep all accounts balanced.
    And what does she think about all day
At the bank? She doesn't think about herself.
What good would that do—now?
And she doesn't have to think about banking.
She's too good at that to think about it.
There's only one thought
That ever crosses her mind: Tomorrow
She'll drive the boy to his summer job at six a.m.
That's what keeps her alive.
She has that to do and think about.
She likes it better even
Than driving him to school in winter,
To the school where she went to school.
It's summer
And they go speeding through the familiar, leafy streets
Of midtown. He mustn't be late to his job!
He's a little man now
And knows already what a whizz *he* is.
Even his perfect record in this summer job
Will follow him through life,
Into all the other parts of town,
Even, at last, downtown.
    But they're always a little late setting out.
Can it be there's something in her
That wants to make him late? What nonsense.
She forgets her keys or her glasses or her cigarettes.
She *has* to have her second cigarette
Along the way, as they go wheeling along.
Sometimes she drops the burning match
On the seat beside her.
Sometimes a hot ash falls

On her skirt, or on his shirt.
The boy is forever brushing at her
Or at himself. She knows he is thinking:
"Next year I'll learn to drive the car myself."
Yes. And what then?
What then will she think about all day?

But suddenly while working late one Friday
She knows.
It had never crossed her mind before.
Her hand trembles on the ledger.
She almost writes out her thought there.
They'll never know what a whizz she *is*.
But maybe *she* will know at last.
Transpose those two figures every month.
They'd never catch her.
Open an account in another name in another bank
In another part of town.
Nobody will know her there,
And she won't know a soul.
She'll be altogether on her own,
Not sent there by someone else
Who discovered too late what a whizz she is.
She lights a cigarette at the very thought!
She brushes the ashes off the ledger
With a clean sweep.
They'll never catch her, never.
She's much too sly for them.
They'll try and try to the very end.
But they'll never catch her till after she's retired
Or maybe dead. Then they'll find all the money
Over in the other bank.
And they'll never know why.
They will look at each other,

Utterly baffled.
And they will ask,
Why did the queer old creature do it?
What need had she to do it?
What need? What need?
They will say,
She has a grown-up son now
Who's made it big
And would surely look after her.
Did she never think of her son
And how it would affect him
And his future
When she transposed those figures
And made the deposits in that other bank?
Did she not stop to think of her son then?
They will ask.
Did she not stop to think of her son?
    She lights another cigarette,
She takes up her pen,
And carefully, thoughtfully,
She begins her first transposing.

Three Heroines

Dedicated to the memory of Lily Heth Dabney, another of my heroines

Dressed to the nines, and she is eighty-six!
A gold lamé gown,
Savage pearls in her pierced earlobes!
Diamonds blazing
That her Grandmother Haynes wore
A century ago!
In Washington City!
Before the War!

The exclamations are all mine, not hers—
And silent. My questions all silent, too:
Who does the woman think she is?
Where does she think she's going in that outfit,
At her age, in her health?
It's not as though *I* don't know, her son,
And *she* doesn't herself know
And the black maid who dresses her, Willie Mae,
And everybody else who cares at all to,
Does not know
In precisely what plot of cemetery ground
This woman will be lying six weeks hence
. . . at most.

"Let me do it," says Willie Mae
About everything. Snapping the golden snaps
As she stands behind her mistress, towering above her,
Towering even in heel-less carpet slippers
("Where does Willie Mae find such slippers any more?"),
Pulling the snaps together with her powerful brown hands,
Pulling the gold cloth over the white powdered back
Of my beautiful mother.
I stand in the doorway, watching, watching,
Waiting in my black tie and dinner jacket
Which I have not worn in ten years till tonight
But which I brought with me on the plane
For her sake, at her request.

And Willie Mae arranging the almost too silvery-white
    mane
(Silvery. Almost like, but not quite like, the blue heads
Of her "less well-bred contemporaries"
With whom she is "reduced to associating"—
So few of her very own sort are left.)
The long silvery-white hair thinned by time and perhaps
    by hats
(Party hats, shopping hats, church hats—
Wide-brimmed hats, cloche hats, turbans,
Whatever the fashion is)
But hair thickened tonight, filled in, ratted by Willie till it
    can deceive
Even me, who remember the old real thickness
The old burnt-umber color, everything, how every hair
And every strand once grew and fell, fell tenderly and
    attentively
Over a child that had mumps or measles
And needed attention
And no doubt once upon a time

Over a lover, a husband.

    And now Willie Mae's handsome hands
Pushing her down onto the dressing-table stool
Like a child. But she is not yielding like a child.
Her knees and her hips yield,
But her posture is unaffected by standing or sitting.
With her long body and short legs she sits
Almost as high as she stands.
When I remark on this, she says,
"A long torso means a long life—
Plenty of room for all the vital organs."
It is one of her jokes.
It is something, in fact, that her Grandmother Haynes used
    to say
About herself, in *her* late eighties, too,
Not before the War, in Washington City
But back in Tennessee, the War over
And everything gone but her diamonds (raked from the
    ashes)
And her flat silver (buried and then a year later exhumed
"Thirty yards N.E. walking in a straight line from the
    sycamore")
And her faded finery, including the black lace mantilla
(From which she was never parted by war or economic
    pestilence),
Proud and witty till the end, that old lady,
Herself finally buried in the shade of that same sycamore,
Proud till the end of what she had endured,
Proud of all she had survived.

    In her gold lamé, my mother recalls it all
And regales us with it one more time, me and Willie Mae.
Seated there on the silk-skirted dressing-table stool

With Willie Mae kneeling before her, sitting
Straight as if corseted, which of course she isn't,
With the false hair Willie has piled on her head
And the false figure just as deceiving
Which Willie also has arranged,
The dress cut low in front, though not so low as to reveal
The old scar from her mastectomy (forty years back
When I was twelve, the operation that she survived
When others were not surviving it.)

    Willie Mae is massaging her miniature feet,
Working them into the miniature gold slippers, tiny feet
But swollen, almost beyond recognition as feet
Until they shall be forcibly shod by the firm hand of Willie
   Mae.
One feels the pain in the room. In one's own feet.
But my mother doesn't bat an eye. Not a wince from her.
Willie hesitates considerably,
Balancing the right slipper lightly in her gentle palm,
Looking up, questioningly.
But Mother, not returning the look, says,
"Go ahead please, Willie Mae."
And herself goes ahead with whatever the funny thing is
She is saying to me.
"There!" Willie Mae says at last. "There you are.
We've got you in them. Now you can go to the ball,
   Cinderella."
And to me: "Ain't she a pretty thing?"
(Archly, knowing how little I like her to play the black-
   nigger).
My mother gazes down at her swollen feet.
"Ah," she sighs. And then suddenly she is laughing:
"This is one Cinderella who won't lose a slipper at the
   ball.

We'll have to take them off with the can opener, Willie
  Mae.''
And Willie laughs so hard she has to hide her face
In her hands, still squatting there. She rocks back and forth.
I *think* she is laughing. I *hope* she is laughing.
Then her frizzy old wig goes askew on her head
And she throws up her hands to hold it on.
She's like a madwoman, there on her haunches
Her whole body throbbing and shaking,
Her big hands holding her head on
. . . And Mother sits very erect, watching her.
Wearing her most serious expression, she watches Willie
  Mae.

  Now we are standing in the narrow side hall, Mother
    and I.
We are almost on our way. The car and driver
Are patient outside in the porte-cochere.
Suddenly I remember where it is we're going.
I'd never thought we'd really go. Not
When she telephoned long-distance and asked I come out
And play her escort: the Golden Wedding Reception
Of a couple she hardly knew the names of.
Still, it was to be at the Club, wasn't it?
Everyone would be there, wouldn't they?
"And I might possibly never go to such a grand affair
Again." Incredible words, I say to myself.
Imagine! But we keep it up, she and I.
And now I see the whole evening before me,
See just how it will be. "Are you sure you want to go,
  Mother?
Are you sure you ought to go, after all?" I ask
With a forced smile, dropping down before her on a
  straight hall chair.

"Why, sure, she ought to go!" cries Willie Mae,
Appearing from nowhere, the Fairy Godmother.
Holding wide the silk-lined mink cape,
She swoops down upon Mother,
Enfolds her in the cape.
For a moment the leathery-brown arms are wrapped
About the lighter brown fur like a belt.
She holds Mother as if she were a baby
In a blanket. She all but kisses her
But doesn't want to spoil the rouged cheek.
She says: "Sure, she ought to go.
My darlin's going to have the time of her life."
Now I am on my feet again.
Mother stares up at me with eyes bright as a child's.
The coloring of her rouge and lipstick seems real—
More than real.
As real as a doll's coloring.
She is more real than life.
She is something Willie Mae has put together
To amuse a sick child with.

It is such a party as one goes to in one's dreams.
That is, in nightmares of a milder sort.
At most there are six faces
In all the vast clutter of faces
Which I think that I can match with names
And in half that number
It is the wrong name I actually come up with.
Yet, sticking like pitch to Mother,
I am smiled upon by everyone.
A faithful son at such an affair as this
Is everybody's hero. And my beautiful mother
Is everybody's heroine. They flock to her
And stand about listening to her famous bon-mots,

Her jokes, her stories. When it is crudely suggested by
    someone
That she might be the oldest person present, she says:
"I don't mind being old;
There's just no future in it."
—A moment's hush, then a burst of laughter.
"Dear lady, with your high-piled silver tresses
And your golden draperies, you are
Like a Greek goddess mingling tonight
Amongst the mere mortals of the Country Club."
—He is "some old professor emeritus
From the University." Or so someone whispers in my ear.
I feel myself blushing. She blinks at him
Twice or three times.
And then, after only a moment's reflection:
"As to my golden draperies—
Greek accusative, Herr Professor—
They are of course in honor of the occasion,
Bought new for our dear friend's wedding anniversary. . . .
Something old—that's me.
Something new—that's the dress.
Something borrowed—that's my son's strength.
Something blue—that's the hair piled so high on my old
    head."

    She is the belle of the ball, without rival.
Everyone comes paying homage to her.
Almost everyone. Only her "medicine man,"
As she calls him, her beloved doctor
Keeps his distance,
He whom we met on the steps outside the Club
And had our exchanges with, brief and awkward,
Out there in the vestibule. I see him eyeing her
From far across the room, and again from a nearer point,

Eyeing her with dark, deep-set eyes
Out of his long, sad face.
Twice at least I see him moving toward her.
He is a man my age. I watch him closely.
Each time he approaches us he lets himself be intercepted,
Averted, drawn aside. How easily
He permits it. How eagerly he greets
Those who intercept him and keep him from us—from
    her.
They, too, no doubt are his aging patients.
But to my mother he will not come. Never.
And of course I have known all along he would not.
From the moment I saw his face
In the dim light on the outside steps I knew.
He looked at her as though he had seen a ghost.
He could not believe his eyes.
She? At such an affair? Dressed to the nines?
With what she had *inside* her?
He gave no sign of recognition.
This woman who resembled his dying patient
Whom he regarded as already dead, really
He would be a fool to mistake the one for the other.
Then, face to face with her
In the bright light of the vestibule
His curt greeting to her is all but insulting.
He cannot help it, though.
He wishes only to turn, with his knowledge,
Back into the uncertain dimness on the steps outside
And on back into the blissful darkness of his primitive
    profession.
What does he know of death? Certainly nothing at all, he
    says to himself.
He knows only about the cessation of life.
She must not ask him to go beyond that with her.
The terror seen in the eyes of most patients

Is no less repulsive to him than its opposite
Whatever the opposite might be called.
There can be no *proper* greeting for death.
There can be no *attitude* at all toward death.
If there is any real way of dealing with death,
Says her beloved doctor to himself,
Then all his success at preventing and relieving pain,
Even at saving life,
Is such a small thing. Hardly worth considering, by com-
     parison.
. . . But the beloved doctor could not turn back into the
     dimness
And he could not brush past my mother in the vestibule.
For one awful moment his eyes met mine.
All that could pass between us was our disbelief—
I don't know of what precisely—and
I don't know which of us
Pitied the other more.
And then the arriving guests
Pushed us on inside and into the party
And parted us. . . . And the evening became an eternity
In which the stricken doctor could not even manage,
Could not *bring* himself
To say goodnight to Mother.

     Home at last, though.
She *bad* done it!
In the car, sitting together in the back seat,
She held my hand tight, never slackening, all the way.
A kind of thing she hadn't done in years,
And then only when I was in trouble,
When I was waiting to face Father
Over my newest act of rebellion
Or my latest incompetence.

The clasp of the hand
Brings it all back:
My foolish first marriage that wasn't really a marriage,
Flunking out of college,
Hitchhiking to the Gulf Coast,
Shipping out work-a-way on a Waterman Line freighter
Never writing them a word about where I was
Then rolling in home
In dirty clothes and too drunk to speak
And finally, worst of all, deserting to the literati.
And then at last forgiveness:
Father forgiving me, because he was dying
(Tears streaming down his cheeks—his only words since
  he could
No longer speak), me forgiving Father because he was dy-
  ing
(Myself speechless too),
Mother forgiving both
And saying there was nothing to forgive.
. . . But all the way home she holds my hand
And talks again of her Grandmother Haynes, only
Of her Grandmother Haynes.

      Of *her* bravery during the War,
Her husband on the Union side,
Off lecturing at Boston and Philadelphia,
Raising money to relieve the suffering
Of loyalist up-country Southerners,
And her own twin brother, the Confederate Senator,
His musical voice and old-fashioned rhetoric
Resounding through the halls of the Capitol at Richmond.
She adored them both, husband and brother,
Wrote each of them a letter every day that passed,
And suffered for them both,

Staying at home with the eleven children and the freed
    slaves,
Persecuted by her neighbors on both sides,
Accused by each side of supporting the other,
Even of spying,
Of sending information from Boston to Richmond
And from Richmond to Boston, and so on to Washington.
Two of her children died, and one freed slave went berserk,
Thought he was Jeff Davis and tried to surrender to *every-
    body*.
But she, Grandmother Haynes, never surrendered
To either side, and never betrayed either side.
She looked after her children, ran the farm,
And gave a dance in the parlor at least once a month.
People said she was vain and frivolous.
She was most assuredly both—and capable and hardwork-
    ing
And brave, too. Toward the end of the War,
Sometime during the last weeks of it,
Her neighbors burned the house and barn,
And even set fire to the summer kitchen and the smoke-
    house.
Then her husband, Grandfather Haynes, came down
And took her and the children through the lines
To Princeton. "It's a pretty place," she wrote her brother.
"To see it, you wouldn't suppose there had been a War."
But now the War was over
She and Grandfather Haynes and the children
Had to go back to Tennessee and be poor as church mice.
They were as poor as if Grandfather Haynes had been on
    the losing side.
All she had was her flat silver and her diamonds and her
    faded finery.
They say she wore her black lace mantilla
To do the milking in.

And her brocades and silks to hoe corn
And chop cotton.
Her husband turned Methodist
And took up preaching seriously,
Preaching religion to the covites
And to the mountain folks and the Black Republicans
"Who were in sore need of it," his wife pronounced.
But she approved. "It's doing good where good is needed,"
She said. "Besides, there's more money in preaching
Than in farming—nowadays." One day her brother, the
    twin,
His whereabouts unknown to her for more than a year,
Appeared in the cowshed doorway
In his cutaway and starched shirtfront,
His silk hat in his hand. He had been to Brazil.
He was on his way out West now, to make a new begin-
    ning,
Traveling under an assumed name: Ben Smith.
"What a pity," she said to him,
"To have to be known as Ben Smith the rest of your life
When you are really Landon Carter of Tennessee."
They embraced, shedding tears for their happy reunion,
As she reported it,
And then parted without tears
But with long looks as he retreated on foot
Out of the barn lot and down the Valley Road,
Both of them knowing they would never meet again
In this life.

    Home at last, yes,
And I have almost forgotten whether
It is my mother I am with
Or my Great-grandmother Haynes.
Though I have heard it all recited before

Time and again, and in the same words,
It never seemed so real.
The two women never seemed so nearly one.
Franklin, her driver, is at her other elbow.
Together, we very nearly carry her inside.
"She was vain and frivolous—and brave,"
Mother says, as much to Franklin as to me.
(Franklin knows the stories, too. He and the good doctor
    together
Have been more son to her than I, in these last years.)
"It's a combination people find it hard to understand.
But they shouldn't. It's not uncommon, do you think?"
Willie is waiting in the lighted doorway.
We traverse that last ten feet
Under the porte-cochere and across the porch.
As we make our way with her
It comes over me how near the end she is.
More than that, it sweeps over me how little even there
    has been
In her life. Wars have raged
Always on the other side of the world for her.
She has not even had to choose
Between neighbors, or not choose.
She did not even have a twin brother
To be torn away from.
Or an idealistic, impractical husband
To stand behind. (Hers was faithful,
Adoring, and a good provider.) Her only child
Never even gave her a scare—not of dying, anyway.
Even his rebellions and desertions and incompetences
Were healthy in their way!
But what is evident somehow
Is that she is every bit the heroine
She would have been had she been called upon to show
Her colors. She has been always ready

And would have been up to whatever
Might have come. And all this she knows! She *knows*.
Yet she is not jaded or disappointed
At not having had her chance to show.
And that, what is that?
Why, that is better than having shown.
It is something more than life.
Death doesn't exist for it, Beloved Doctor.

Just inside the door to the side hall, Willie
Is waiting. She does not take one step forward.
She waits in her self-appointed place
For us to deliver our charge.
She does not even open her arms
Until we are in the doorway and standing before her.
Then she throws wide her arms and clasps her mistress to
  her bosom
As though she were herself the angel waiting on the other
  side.
"My honey, my darlin'," she says, hugging her, petting
  her.
And I hear Mother's muffled voice: "Willie Mae, I'm so
  tired."

"Of course. Sure you are," says Willie Mae.
I stand there beside Franklin, feeling empty-handed.
There is nothing else for me to do.
"I'll put up the car," says Franklin. He is lucky.
And he leaves me alone with just Mother and Willie Mae.
"Maybe she ought not to have gone, after all," I say,
Not knowing anything else to say.
"She *had* to go," Willie says.
"I think she had a wonderful time," I say,
Not thinking of anything else to say.

"Of *course* she had a wonderful time,"
Says Willie, still holding Mother, and looks at me over
  Mother's head.
As if to say, What *else* did you expect of *her*?
"Anyway, I'm glad you waited up for her," I say.
And Willie, with a look of even deeper wonder,
Asks with her eyes: What else did you expect of *me*?

In the Miro District

WHAT I MOST OFTEN THINK ABOUT WHEN I
am lying awake in the night, or when I am taking a long
automobile trip alone, is my two parents and my maternal
grandfather. I used to suppose, after I had first got to be a
grown man and had first managed to get away from Tennessee, that those two parents of mine thrusting my grandfather's company upon me as they did when I was growing
up, and my company upon him when he was growing very
old, and their asking the two of us to like it, though we
possessed the very opposite natures, was but that couple's
ruthless method of disposing of the two of us, child and
aging parent, in one blow. But I can see now—from the
vantage point of my own late middle age—that there was
really no ruthlessness in it on their part. Because I realize
that living their busy, genteel, contented life together in the
1920s they didn't have the slightest concept of what that
old man my grandfather was like. Or of what that boy,
their son, was like either. (Of what the one's past life had
been or of what the other's would be like in the future.)
They weren't people to speculate about what other people
and other times were "like." They knew only that what
they did was what everybody else still did about grandfathers and grandsons in or about the year 1925—in and
around Nashville, Tennessee.

The fact is, my two parents were destined to go to their

graves never suspecting that they had put a grandfather and a grandson in so false a position with each other that the boy and the old man would one day have to have it out between them. Indeed, they would go to their graves never suspecting that long before either of them had ever given a serious thought to dying, Grandfather and I had already had it out between us quite brutally and fatefully and had it out, as a matter of fact, in the front hall of their house in Acklen Park, in Nashville.

It happened the summer when my grandfather was seventy-nine and I had just turned eighteen. Any real pretense at companionship between the old man and me came to an abrupt and unhappy end that summer. It left me with complications of feeling that nothing else had ever done. For my grandfather, of course, whose story this is meant to be—more than mine—it did something considerably worse than leave him with complications of feeling.

What actually happened was that he turned up at our house in Acklen Park one day in July, driving his Dodge touring car and wearing his gabardine topcoat and his big straw hat, arrived there unheralded and unannounced, as he himself was fond of saying, and let himself in our front door with his own key, the key which, despite his protests, my two parents always insisted upon his having. And what he found inside the house that day was not a clean-cut young boy whom he had watched growing up and whom his daughter and son-in-law—away then on a short summer trip—had left at home to see after the premises. He found, instead, a disheveled, disreputable-looking young fellow of eighteen summers who was hardly recognizable to his own grandfather, a boy who had just now frantically pulled on his clothes and who instead of occupying his parents' house alone was keeping a young girl in the house with him, a girl whom he had hurriedly hidden—at the first sound of his grandfather's tires in the driveway—hidden, as a matter of fact, in the big oak wardrobe of the downstairs bedroom which his visiting grandfather was always expected to occupy. The ensuing confrontation between the grandfather and the grandson seemed on its surface to be accidental and something that might finally be forgotten by both of them. But it was not quite so simple as that. . . . Neither the old man nor his grandson was ever quite the same after that day—not the same with each other and probably not the same within themselves. Whatever their old relationship had been, it was over forever.

TO ME IT SEEMS NATURAL THAT I SHOULD think about all of this whenever I am lying awake at night or when I am behind the wheel of my car on some endless highway. The memory of it raises questions in my mind that there seem to be no answers to; and those are inevitably the questions one entertains at such times. I find myself wondering why, in that quaint Tennessee world I grew up in, it was so well established that grandfathers and grandsons were to be paired off and held answerable to each other for companionship; why it was that an old graybeard and a towheaded little boy, in that day and age, were expected to be more companionable even than fathers and sons are told today they ought to be. For it really is my recollection that anywhere one turned in that world one was apt to see a bent old man and a stiff-necked little boy—trudging along a country road together or plodding along the main street of a town. The world I am speaking of isn't the hard-bitten, monkey-trial world of East Tennessee that everybody knows about, but a gentler world in Middle Tennessee and more particularly the little region around Nashville which was known fifty years ago as the Nashville Basin and which in still earlier times, to the first settlers— our ancestors—was known somewhat romantically perhaps, and ironically, and incorrectly even, as the Miro District.

I must digress here to say something about why that region around Nashville was so designated, because it has something or other to do with this story. My grandfather, who did not take Nashville so seriously as my parents did, was fond of referring to the city itself as the Miro District (because he said only an antique Spanish name could do justice to the grandeur which Nashvillians claimed for themselves). According to Grandfather this region had originally been so called in honor of one Don Estevan Miro, last of the Spanish governors of Spanish Louisiana, and according to this same knowledgeable grandfather of mine, the entire state of Tennessee had once been claimed to be a rightful part of that province by both the French and the Spanish, in their day as its rulers. He used often to say to me, all irony about grandeur aside, that knowing such odd pieces of history about the place where one lived made the life one lived there seem less boring. He didn't couch it quite that way. He would not, of course, have used the word *boring*. It wasn't in his vocabulary. But there is no doubt that's what he meant. And I used to try to imagine why it was that when he was scouting through the low ground or hill country west of the Tennessee River during the Civil War, it made the War seem less hateful to him at times and less scary and less boring for him to know— or to believe—that the Spanish and the French had once held title to what was by then his own country or that the Indians had once held that land sacred, or for him to realize whenever he came in to Nashville that the site of the old citadel itself, Fort Nashborough, had once actually been known merely as Frenchman's Lick.

My grandfather, when I first remember him, lived over in the next county from us, forty miles west of Nashville. But he was always and forever driving over for those visits of his—visits of three or four days, or longer—transporting himself back and forth from Hunt County to Nashville in his big tan touring car, with the canvas top put back in almost all weather, and usually wearing a broad-brimmed hat—a straw in summer, a felt in winter—and an ankle-length gabardine topcoat no matter what the season was.

He was my maternal grandfather and was known to everyone as Major Basil Manley. Seeing Major Manley like that at the wheel of his tan touring car, swinging into our driveway, it wasn't hard to imagine how he had once looked riding horseback or muleback through the wilds of West Tennessee when he was a young boy in Forrest's cavalry, or how he had looked, for that matter, in 1912, nearly half a century after he had ridden with General Forrest, at the time when he escaped from a band of hooded nightriders who had kidnapped him then—him and his law partner (and who had murdered his law partner before his eyes, on the banks of Bayou du Chien, near Reelfoot Lake).

Even when I was a very small boy, I always dreaded the sight of him out there in our driveway in his old car when he was arriving for a visit. I hated the first sound of his tires in the gravel as he came wheeling up to the house and then suddenly bore down on the brakes at the foot of our front porch steps. I dreaded him not because I was frightened by his coming or by the history of his violent exploits, which I knew about from an early time, but because I was aware always of the painful hours that he and I, who had nothing in common and for whom all our encounters were a torture, would be expected to put in together.

The old man had always had a way of turning up, you see—even when I was little more than an infant—just when it suited *me* least, when I had *other* plans which might include almost anything else in the world but the presence of a grandfather with whom it was intended I should be companionable. Sometimes he would go directly into our back yard, if it were summertime, without even removing his hat or his gabardine coat. He would plant one of the canvas yard chairs on the very spot where I had been building a little airfield or a horse farm in the grass. Then he would throw himself down into the chair and undo his collar button and remove his starched collar—he seldom wore a tie in those days—and next he would pull his straw hat down over his face and begin his inevitable dialogue with me without our having exchanged so much as a glance or a how-do-you-do. It used to seem to me he only knew I was there with him because he knew I was required to be there. "I guess you've been behaving yourself," he said from under his hat, "the way a Nashville boy ought to behave himself." . . . And, of course, I knew well enough what was meant by that. It meant I was some kind of effeminate city boy who was never willing to visit his grandfather alone in the country and who could never comprehend what it would be to ride muleback through the wilds of West Tennessee—either in pursuit of Yankee marauders or in flight from hooded nightriders. Looking up at the old man from the grass beside his chair (or from the carpet beside his platform rocker if we were settled in his downstairs bedroom), I thought to myself—thought this, or something like it—Someday you and I will have to have it out between us. I shall have to show you how it is with me and how I could never be what you are. . . . I often looked up at him, wanting—I know now—to say something that would insult him and make him leave me alone or make him take his walking stick to me. The trouble was, of course—and I seemed to have sensed this before I was school age even—that we couldn't understand or care anything about each other. Something in each of us forbade it. It was as though we faced each other across the distasteful present, across a queer, quaint world that neither of us felt himself a part of.

When I looked up at him while we were talking, often out in the back yard but more often in his room, I could never think exactly what it was about him that I hated or if I really hated him at all. Yet many a time I had that shameful feeling of wanting to insult him. And so I got into the habit of trying to see him as my two parents saw him. That's the awful part, really. I would look at him until I saw him as I knew they saw him: an old country granddaddy who came to town not wearing a tie and with only a bright gold collar button shining where a tie ought to have been in evidence. It seems shocking to me nowadays how well I knew at that tender age just how my parents did surely see such an old man and, indeed, how they saw all else in the world about us. They saw everything in terms of Acklen Park in the city of Nashville in the Nashville Basin in Middle Tennessee in the old Miro District as it had come to be in the first quarter of the twentieth century. I suppose it was my knowing how Mother and Father saw the other grandfathers who did actually live with *their* families in the Acklen Park neighborhood that made me know for certain how they saw Major Basil Manley. To them, those other grandfathers seemed all elegance while he seemed all roughness. Those others lived quietly with their sons and daughters while he insisted upon living apart and in a county that was only on the periphery of Middle Tennessee. Those other grandfathers were a part of the families who had taken them in. (They had managed to become so or perhaps had always been so.) When you saw one of those other grandfathers out walking with a little grandson along West End Avenue, it was apparent at once that the two of them were made of the same clay or at least that their mutual aim in life was to make it appear to the world that they were. Sometimes the old man and the little boy walked along West End hand in hand or sometimes with their arms about each other, the old man's arm on the little boy's shoulder, the little boy's arm about the old man's waist. It is a picture that comes into my mind almost every day that I live.

THIS ANCIENT AND WELL-ESTABLISHED practice of pairing off young with old so relentlessly and so exclusively had, I think—or *has*—as one of its results in Nashville the marvel that men over fifty whom one meets there nowadays are likely to seem much too old-fashioned to be believed in almost—much too stiff in their manner to be taken seriously at all. They seem to be putting on an act. It is as if they are trying to *be* their grandfathers. Either that or these grandsons of Confederate veterans are apt to have become pathetic old roués and alcoholics, outrageously profane, and always willing to talk your ear off in the Country Club bar—usually late at night—about how far they have fallen away from their ideals, about how very different they are from the men their grandfathers were. To hear them talk, one would actually suppose none of them ever had a father. One gets the impression that they only had elegant grandfathers, born before 1860.

What is more to the point, though, is that this business of pairing off bent old men with stiff-necked little boys plainly had its effect, too, upon the old men—the old grandfathers themselves. For when finally they reached extreme old age either they became absurd martinets, ordering the younger men and boys in their families about in their quavery old voices (and often getting laughed at behind their backs) or some among these very same old men who had once stood firm at Missionary Ridge or had fought in the trenches before Petersburg or, like Grandfather Manley, had ridden with General Forrest became toward the very end as thoroughly domesticated as any old woman—could be seen fussing about the house like some old spinster great-aunt, rearranging the furniture or washing up little stacks of dishes, forever petting and hugging the young people in the family or clucking and fretting and even weeping softly whenever the young people didn't behave themselves as they ought to do.

My Grandfather Manley was an exception to all of this, and I had been fully aware of the fact long before the time he caught me and my girl staying in his room. He was an exception in the first place because he refused from the very start to move into the same house with my mother and father—at the time when he was widowed—or even, for that matter, to come and live in the same town with us. He had resisted making that fatal mistake which so many of his contemporaries made—of moving in with their children. He was clearly different from them in a number of other respects, too, but it must have been that first, firm refusal of his to move in with us that allowed him to think for a few years that he could altogether escape the ignominious fate—of the one kind or the other—which his contemporaries had to endure.

He did not turn into an old woman and he did not try to play the martinet. Except for those relatively brief visits of his, he was free of the rules and mores of my parents' Nashville life. After three or four days spent mostly in my company, he would be off again to his farm in Hunt County and to the "primitive" life he lived there. If it was hard for anyone to see why he insisted on living in Hunt County when he could have lived so comfortably in Nashville, I at any rate thanked God on my knees that he had made that choice and prayed that he would never change his mind. For the most part, he went on living in the drafty, unheated farmhouse that he and his father before him had been born in. And on a farm where both cotton and tobacco had once been the money crops, but where truck farming had now become more profitable. There was no prestige or tradition about the kind of farming he did over there. (It was somehow felt an embarrassment that he raised only tomatoes, strawberries, corn. It amounted to *truck* farming, though we did not even say the word.) And certainly there was no romance about the place itself. That is to say, his farm and the county it was in were considered somewhat beyond the pale, not being in the handsome, bluegrass, limestone country where livestock farms—and particularly horse farms—made the landscape a joy to look upon and where the people had always held themselves well above other mortal Tennesseeans. He preferred to go on living over there even after my father had bought our fine house in Acklen Park and set aside the room there for his exclusive occupancy.

IT WILL BE USEFUL AT THIS POINT TO EX-plain that before that day when I hid my girl in the wardrobe, there actually had been two other serious and quite similar face-offs between my grandfather and me, and useful that I give some account of those earlier confrontations. They both took place in the very same year as the fateful one in the front hall. And on both of those occasions Grandfather stayed on in the house afterward, just as if nothing out of the ordinary had happened. This was so despite there having been more violent interplay between us—verbal and otherwise—in those two encounters than there was destined to be in the last.

The first of them was in April of that year. My parents were not out of town that time. Rather, my father was in the hospital to undergo an operation on his prostrate gland. He went into the hospital on the Sunday afternoon before the Monday morning when the operation was scheduled. Possibly he and my mother regarded the operation more apprehensively than they should have. My mother managed to obtain a room next to his in the hospital. She went in with him on Sunday in order to be near him during that night. My grandfather had of course been notified of the circumstances. Mother had even made a long-distance telephone call from Nashville to Huntsboro. And since Grandfather declined still to have a telephone in his house or to let the lines to other houses go across his land, he had had to be fetched by a messenger from his farm to Central's office on the town square.

That was on Saturday afternoon, and Mother had hoped he might come to Nashville on Sunday and stay in the house—presumably to keep me company—at least until Father was safely through the operation. But the old man was offended by everything about the situation. He resented being sent for and brought to the telephone office. He resented having to hear Mother's indelicate news in the presence of Central herself (a local girl and a cousin of ours). And the worst of it was, so he said on the telephone to Mother, he didn't believe in the seriousness of the operation. Actually, when Mother and Father had previously mentioned to him the possibility of such surgery, he had insisted that no such operation "existed" and that the doctor was pulling Father's leg. I was told this afterward by my father—long afterward—who said the old man had clearly resented such an unseemly subject's being referred to in his presence by his daughter or even by his son-in-law.

Anyhow, my mother told me that Grandfather would not be coming to stay with me on Sunday. I don't know whether or not she believed it. And I cannot honestly say for sure whether or not *I* believed he wasn't coming. I know only that on that Sunday afternoon, after my parents had left for the hospital, I telephoned two of my friends, two Acklen Park boys who would be graduating with me from Wallace School that June, and invited them to come over and to bring with them whatever they might have managed to filch from their fathers' liquor closets. Actually, it was only my way of informing them of what I had in mind for that Sunday afternoon and evening, because I knew where the key to Father's closet was and knew there was more than enough bourbon whiskey there to suffice for three boys on their first real binge. Since this was an opportunity we had all been contemplating for some time, my invitation was only a matter of form.

I heard Grandfather Manley in the driveway at about half past six. In fact I had lost track of time by then. We had been gulping down our whiskey as though it were lemonade. I could hardly stand on my feet when he came into the breakfast room, where we were seated about the table. I had made a stab at getting up when I first heard his car outside. My intention was to meet him, as usual, in the front hall. But as soon as I had got halfway up I felt a little sick. I knew I would be too unsteady on my feet to effect my usual sort of welcome in the hall, which would have entailed my taking his bag to his room for him and helping him off with his topcoat. Instead, I was still seated at the table when he stepped into the breakfast-room doorway. I did manage to rise from my chair then, scraping it crazily along the linoleum floor, which, at any rate, was more than the other two boys managed. And I faced him across the gold pocket watch that he was now holding out in his open palm like a piece of incriminating evidence. Although I say I faced him across the watch, his eyes were not really on me when he spoke but on the other boys at the table. "It's more than half an hour past my supper-time," he said. "I generally eat at six." This is how I can account for the time it was. Drunk as my two friends assuredly were and difficult as they undoubtedly found it to rise, they did, when Grandfather said that about supper-time, manage to rise somehow from their chairs and without a word of farewell went stumbling out through the kitchen and out of the house.

Grandfather then turned and went to his room, giving

me an opportunity to put away the liquor and the glasses. Or I suppose that was his purpose. Perhaps he had only gone to remove his topcoat and his hat. When he came back, I had not stirred but still sat there with one hand on the quart bottle, fully intending to pour myself another drink. I had waited, I think, with the intention of pouring it in his presence. Looking at me, he said, "It's a fine sort of company you are keeping nowadays here in Nashville." At that I took up the bottle and began pouring whiskey into my glass.

"They're my friends," I said, not looking at him. He stepped over to the table, seized the bottle by its neck with one hand, and took hold of my glass with the other. But I held on firmly to each—did so for several moments, that is. Together we were supporting both glass and bottle in mid-air. And then it must have been simultaneously that each of us relinquished his hold on both. The glass fell to the table, crashing and breaking into small pieces and splashing its contents over the tabletop. The bottle landed sidewise on the table, spewing out whiskey on Grandfather Manley's trousers, then rolled onto the floor, coming to rest there, unbroken but altogether empty. Immediately Grandfather Manley said, "Now you get that mess cleaned up." And he went off through the house to his room again.

His command had literally a sobering effect upon me, as probably nothing else could have done—more so, certainly, than the breakage and spillage had. Though I was feeling unsteady, I did clean up the tabletop and I wiped up the floor. I decided to take the fragments of glass and the empty bottle out to the garbage can in the alley. I didn't want my mother to see any of it and to raise questions when she came home on Monday. As I was returning from the garbage can to the house through the dark back yard, I had sudden guilt feelings about my mother and father, visualizing them in the hospital, Father lying in the white bed and Mother sitting in a straight chair beside him. I knew that I had to go to my grandfather's room and take whatever satisfaction I could from the scolding I fancied he would surely give me.

I found him in his room, seated in his platform rocker, which like all the other furniture in the room was made of golden oak—with caning in the seat and back. He sat in it as if it were a straight chair, with one of his long, khaki-clad legs crossed stiffly over the other and one high-topped brown shoe sticking out assertively into the room. All the furniture in the room was furniture which he had brought there, at my mother's urging, from his house in Hunt County. It was in marked contrast with the rest of the furniture in our house. Mother had said, however, that he would feel more comfortable and at home with his own things in the room, and that he would be more likely to take real possession of it—which, after all, was what she and Father hoped for. I suspect they thought that would be a first step toward moving him in to live with us. In the end, Mother was actually disappointed at the particular pieces he chose to bring. But there will be a time later on for me to say more about that.

Anyway, there he was in his rocker, already divested of his starched collar and of the vest he always wore under his gabardine coat. His suspenders were loosened and hanging down over the arms of the chair. And he had lit his first cigarette of the evening. (He had given up his pipe at the time of his escape from the nightriders and had taken up cigarettes, instead, because he said they gave more relief to his nerves. He had given up his beard and mustache then, too, because he couldn't forget how awful they had smelt to him when he had been hiding in the swamp for days on end and under stagnant water for many hours of the time.) I came into the room and stood before him, my back to the great golden-oak folding bed, which, when it was folded away against the wall, as it was now, could easily be mistaken for a large wardrobe like the one I was facing on the other side of the room, and matching it almost exactly in size, bulk, and color. I stood there in silence for several moments, waiting for him to begin the kind of dressing-down which he had never given me and which if he could have given me then might have made all the difference in the world in our future relation—and perhaps our lives.

For a while he said nothing. Then he said, "I don't want any supper tonight. If the cook left something, you'd better go eat it. Because if you *can* eat, it will likely do you good!" There was no note of sympathy in his voice, only an acknowledgment of my condition. But I could tell there was going to be no dressing-down, either. It was going to be just like always before when we had been left alone together.

"I can't eat anything," I said. And I began to feel that I was going to be actively ill. But somehow I was able to control and overcome that feeling. Then I began to feel drunk again, as drunk as I had been when he first came in on us. I slumped down onto a leather ottoman and sat with my elbows on my knees, still looking at him. It was just as it had always been before. We had nothing to say to each other—nothing we *could* say. And thinking about all the times we had been left together like this when I was a little boy, it seemed to me that I had always been somewhat drunk whenever he and I had had to talk, and had always been unable to make any sense at all. "Tell me what it was like," I suddenly began now in a too loud voice. "Tell me what it was like to be kidnapped by those night-riders . . . out in Lake County." He sat forward in his chair as if so astonished by what I had said that he would have to come to his feet. But still he didn't get up, and I went on. "And what it was like . . . to see Captain Tyree hanged before your very eyes." I was hesitating and stammering as I spoke. I had never before said anything like this to him. In the past, you see, when we had been wanting a topic, I had always pressed him to tell me about the Civil War—not because I cared much about the War but because, as I realize now but didn't understand then, it was what my parents cared about and were always telling me I ought to get him to talk about. But he didn't want to talk about the War. Not in a serious way. He would say, "There's little to tell, God knows," and put me off with a slapstick anecdote or two, about shooting a man's hat off during the raid on Memphis, outside the Gayoso Hotel, or about meeting General Forrest on a back-country road when, as a boy of sixteen and riding bareback on a mule, he was on his way to enlist in Forrest's own critter company, how General Forrest and some other officers had forced him off the road and into a muddy ditch and didn't even look back at him until he yelled out after them every filthy kind of thing he could think of. "But since I was a mite small for my age," he would say, "they must have mistook me for some local farm boy. Only Forrest himself ever looked back—looked back with that sickly grin of his." And then he was sure to end that anecdote saying, "Likely I'm the onliest man or boy who ever called Bedford Forrest a son-of-a-bitch and lived."

That was not, of course, the kind of war story I wanted. My father, who read Civil War history, would, in my presence, try to draw the old man out on the subject, asking him about Forrest's strategy or whether or not the War might have been won if Jeff Davis had paid more attention to the "Western Theatre." And all Grandfather Manley would say was: "I don't know about any of that. I don't know what it matters."

But that Sunday night in his room, instead of plaguing him to talk about the War as I had always previously tended to do, I took the opposite tack. And I think I could not have stopped myself from going on even if I had wanted to. As I rattled on, I felt my grandfather looking at me uncertainly, as though he were not sure whether it was I or he that was drunk. "Tell me about your kidnapping," I said, actually wavering on the big leather ottoman as I spoke, and my voice rising and lowering—quite beyond my control. "Or tell me about the earthquake in 1811 that your old daddy used to tell you about, that made the Mississippi River run upstream and formed Reelfoot Lake, and how you imagined when you were lost in the swamp and half out of your head that you could see the craters and fissures from the earthquake still there." Suddenly Grandfather lit his second cigarette, got up from his chair, and went over and stood by a window. I suppose it occurred to him that I was mocking him, though I couldn't have said, myself, whether or not I was. "You're all worked up," he said. "And it's not just that whiskey in you. Your mother's got you all worked up about this damnable operation of your dad's."

"Tell me what it was like," I began again. In my confused and intoxicated state, my whole system seemed determined to give it all back to him—all the scary stories I had listened to through all the years about the nightriders of Reelfoot Lake. I can hear myself clearly even now, sometimes speaking to him in a singsongy voice more like a child's voice than the ordinary man's voice I had long since acquired. "Tell me what it was like to wake up in the Walnut Log Hotel at Samburg, Tennessee. . . . Tell me what it was like to lie in your bed in that shackly, one-story, backwoods hotel and have it come over you that it was no dream, that hooded men on horseback filled the yard outside, each with a blazing pine-knot torch, that there really was at every unglazed window of your room the raw rim of a shotgun barrel."

* * *

I HEAR MYSELF GOING ON AND ON THAT
Sunday night. As I babbled away, it was not just that night
but every night that I had ever been alone in the house
with him. I had the sensation of retching or of actually
vomiting, not the whiskey I had in my stomach but all the
words about the nightriders I had ever had from him and
had not known how to digest—words I had not ever wanted
to hear. My confusion was such that some of the time I
did not know at all what I was saying. I knew only that
this was the beginning of my freedom from him. And I
had no notion of why it should be so. Only now and then
a vague thought or an image took shape for me—of him as
the young soldier on horseback or of the War itself that he
would not reveal to us, that he always substituted talk about
the nightriders for. But now I would not have to have any
of the nightrider business again. I was giving it all back.
And as I did so, how nerve-racking my voice was, almost
beyond endurance—to me no less than to my grandfather,
he who sat before me in the bright light he had now put
on in the room, wearing his rough country clothes, his blue
shirt and khaki trousers, blinking his veiny eyelids at me,
not really listening any longer to what I said. He was thinking then, as I knew he had always thought: *You don't want
to hear such stuff as that. Not from me, you don't. You just
want to hear yourself sketching in my old stories, giving them
back to me. It makes you feel good. It helps you hide your
feelings or whatever it is you've always wished to hide.* He sat
before me blinking and thinking, one process, or one
rhythm at any rate. And not really listening to me at all.

But I couldn't stop myself, any more than he could stop
me with his blinking or with the twisting back and forth
of his weak chin and lean jaw. The twisting was somehow
offensive to me. It was something I had seen him do to
other people who troubled or annoyed him in some way.

It was almost as if he were chewing tobacco and looking for a place to spit—which is something he liked to boast he had never done. And I heard my awful childlike voice going on. It was as though it were not mine and as though I were someone hidden on the far side of the room from us in the big oak wardrobe where I would one day hide that girl. But my voice persisted. I went on and on, so nervous as I looked into his white-blue eyes that I feared I should burst into tears, or, worse still, into silly, little-boy laughter.

"Tell how they ordered you and Marcus Tyree out of your beds though you each slept with a revolver at your side, ordered you up from the straw mattresses on those homemade bedsteads and required the two of you to get fully dressed, even to putting on your starched collars and your black shoestring ties, and then escorted you both on muleback, at gunpoint, out to the edge of the bayou."

But he said nothing. He only kept on blinking at me. And the bright light had little or nothing to do with it. In recent years he had always blinked at me. (When I was fourteen, when I was sixteen, when I was eighteen. Those were the years when it got to be unbearable.) Each time we met, I pressed him to tell me tales about his war exploits and the suffering he endured. ("Ask him!" my father had said to me. "Ask him!" my mother had said to me.) That was what set him blinking usually. He distrusted all garrulous young people. Most of all, those who asked questions. *Why have you never waited and allowed me to speak for myself?* I knew he was thinking, but didn't say. *And why is it you've never opened your mouth to me about yourself?*

He had always thought I was hiding something. Tonight his suspicion was so strong I could hear it in his breathing. I went on and on. "Tell me again how you, alone, escaped! How the nightriders made a bonfire on the banks of the bayou and put a rope around Captain Tyree's neck, torturing him, pulling him up and letting him down until finally he said, 'Gentlemen, you're killing me.' And then one of the men said, 'That's what we aim to do, Captain.' And they yanked him up for the last time. How a moment later, when all eyes were on the strung-up body of your friend, your law partner, your old comrade-in-arms from the War days and with whom you had come there only as 'two friends of the court' to settle old land disputes made not by any man on earth but by an earthquake a hundred years before almost to the day, how at that moment, really in one of your wicked explosions of temper—afterward it was your rage you remembered most clearly—you vowed to survive (vowed it in your rage) and yourself bring to justice those squatters-turned-outlaws. And seeing your one chance to escape, you, in your saving rage, dived into the brackish water of the Bayou du Chien—you a man of sixty and more even then. Tell me how . . . you hid under the log floating in the bayou (somebody made a gavel from its wood for you later) and how in the pre-dawn dark they filled the dead log you were under full of buckshot, supposing it was you that was dead out there, supposing it was your body they saw floating, drifting sluggishly in the Bayou du Chien toward Reelfoot Lake. But all the while—"

Before I finished, he had begun to laugh his sardonic courtroom laugh, which was more like an old piece of farm machinery that needed oiling than like most human laughter. It was a laugh that was famous for having destroyed the case of many a courtroom lawyer in Hunt County—more frequently than any argument or rhetoric he had ever employed. I had heard him laugh that way at our dinner table, too, when my father had expressed some opinion or theory that Grandfather had not agreed with but that he knew he could not refute with logic. And I went on long after I knew that any use there might have been in my performance that day was over. Long after I had realized that if my performance were going to have any effect, it had already been had. At some point I could see that he was no longer listening and that, after all, the victory of this engagement was somehow his. Finally I was silenced by his silence. Now he had come back from the window and sat down in the chair again and was smiling his wickedest courtroom smile at me. His green eyes seemed very bright, and I could tell that for a few moments at least my singsongy recounting of his experiences had stirred his memory. I felt that if I encouraged him—and if he permitted himself—he would even now take up where I had left off and describe one more time his ten days of wandering in the swamp after his escape and then perhaps his finally reaching a logging road on high ground and there lapping up water like an Indian out of the hoofprints of horses because he knew it was rainwater and pure, and then the ride to Tiptonville, concealed under the hay in a farmer's wagon bed.

And at last the trial of the nine nightriders.

He loved to dwell upon the fact that all nine men were proved to be previously convicted criminals, not downtrodden backwoodsmen whose livelihood in fishing and hunting the government and the big landowners of Lake County wished to take away. Perhaps he went over all that in his mind for a few moments, but what his wicked smile and the light in his eyes spoke of was a victory he was reveling in at that present moment. My long spiel about the nightrider trouble had reflected the many times I had had to listen to his account of it. And to him, I somehow understood in a flash of insight, it meant above all else what was perhaps dearest to his soul of all things during those years. It meant how many times he had successfully avoided reminiscing about the War. In retrospect I can see that it had become almost mechanical with him to answer any requests I made for stories about the War with stories about his adventures at Reelfoot Lake. For a number of years, I think, he had tried to distract me with just any of his old stories about hunting bear or deer or about lawsuits he had had that took him into tough communities where he had sometimes to fight his way out of the courtroom and sometimes share a bed in a country hotel with a known murderer whom he was defending. But for a time there had been no variations to his response. I did not know then, and do not know now, at what moment he took a vow never to talk about the Civil War and his own experiences in it, whether he unconsciously and gradually began to avoid the subject with members of his family—after he had already ceased talking about it with anybody else. But from his smile that day and his laughter, which I had only before heard him direct at my parents, I began to sense that he regarded me chiefly as their agent and that yielding to me in my pressing him to tell me about his war would be the first chink in his armor of resistance to my parents and could end with nothing less than their bringing him into Nashville and into our house to live.

At last he got up from his chair again. He was no longer smiling at me but clearly he was no longer angry with me, either. And at the end, when he dismissed me from his room, it occurred to me that seeing an eighteen-year-old boy drunk was nothing new to a man of his experience in the rough sort of world he came along in and that my pilfering my father's whiskey while he was in the hospital seemed to him almost a natural and inevitable mistake for a boy my age to have made. "You've had a hard day," he said—rather sternly but not more so than if he had been correcting me about some show of bad manners. "Get yourself a night's sleep, and we'll go to the hospital tomorrow to see how your dad is making out. Seems to me he and your mama's got you so worked up there's no telling what you *might* have done if I hadn't shown up as I did, unheralded and unannounced."

IT WAS HARDLY SIX WEEKS LATER THAT WE had our second run-in. He came in to Nashville on Decoration Day, when, of course, the Confederate veterans always held their most elaborate services and celebrations out at the State Fairground. Father and Mother had gone to Memphis to visit Father's sister out there over the Decoration Day weekend. They wouldn't have planned to go, so they said, except that Grandfather as usual swore he was never again going to attend a Confederate Reunion of any kind. He had been saying for years that all the reunions amounted to were occasions to promote everybody to a higher rank. He acknowledged that once upon a time he had been a party to this practice. He had been so for many years, in fact. But enough was enough. It was one thing to promote men like himself who had been private soldiers to the rank of captain and major but quite another to make them colonels and generals. They had voted him his majority back in the years before his kidnapping by the nightriders. But since the experience of that abduction by those murderous backwoodsmen, he had never attended another Confederate Reunion. For more than a dozen years now he had insisted that it would not be possible for him to pass in through the Fairground gates on any Decoration Day without being sure to come out with the rank of colonel. He could not countenance that. And he could not countenance that gathering of men each year to repeat and enlarge upon reminiscences of something that he was beginning to doubt had ever had any reality.

From the first moment after I had put my parents on the train for Memphis, I think I knew how that weekend was going to go. I would not have admitted it to myself and didn't admit it for many years afterward. I suspect, too, that from the time some weeks earlier when he had heard of my parents' plans to go to Memphis—that is, assuming that he would not be coming in for the Reunion—Grandfather must also have had some idea of how it might go. Looking back, it seems almost as if he and I were plotting the whole business together.

It didn't of course seem that way at the time. Naturally, I can only speculate on how it seemed for him, but he had made more than one visit to Nashville since the day he found me there drinking with my friends, and I had observed a decided change in him—in his attitude toward me, that is. On one occasion he had offered me a cigarette, which was the next thing, it seemed to me then, to offering me a drink. I knew of course that Grandfather had, at one time or another, used tobacco in most of its forms. And we all knew, as a matter of fact, that when he closed the door to his room at night he nearly always poured himself a drink—poured it into a little collapsible tumbler that, along with his bottle of sourmash, he had brought with him in his Gladstone bag. His drinking habits had never been exactly a secret, though he seldom made any direct reference to them except in certain stories he told. And whatever changes there were in his style during his very last years, his drinking habits never changed at all—not, I believe, from the time when he was a young boy in the Confederate Army until the day he died.

It is true that I often smelt liquor on his breath when he arrived at our house for a visit, but I believe that was because he made a habit of having a quick one when he stopped—along the way—to rest and to relieve himself at the roadside. Moreover, that was only like the drink he had in his room at night—for his nerves. I believe the other drinking he had done in his lifetime consisted entirely of great bouts he had sometimes had with groups of men on hunting trips, often as not in that very region around Reelfoot Lake where he had witnessed the torture and strangulation of his old comrade-in-arms and law partner and where he had later wandered for ten nights in the swampy woodland thereabout (he had regarded it as unsafe to travel by day and unsafe to knock on any cabin door, lest it be the hideaway of one of the nightriders), wandered without food and without fresh water to drink, and suffering sometimes from hallucinations.

I feel that I must digress again here in order to say a few things about those hallucinations he had; which must actually have been not unlike delirium tremens, and about impressions that I myself had of that country around the Lake when I visited it as a child. Actually, as a very young child—no more than three or four years old—I had been taken on a duck-hunting trip to the Lake with Father and Grandfather and a party of other men from Hunt County. I didn't go out with them, of course, when, decked out in their grass hats and grass skirts and capes—for camouflage—they took up their positions in the marshlands. I was left in the hunting lodge on the lake's edge in the care of the Negro man who had been brought along to do the cooking. I don't remember much about the days or the nights of that expedition. I must have passed them comfortably and happily enough. All I remember clearly is what seemed the endless and desolate periods of time I spent during the early-morning hours and twilight hours of each day of our stay there, all alone in the lodge with Thomas, the cook. As I sat alone on the screened porch, which went all the way round that little batten-board lodge (of no more than three or four rooms and a loft) and listened to Thomas's doleful singing in the kitchen, all I could see in any direction was the dark water of the lake on one side and of the bayou on the other, with the cypress stumps and other broken trees rising lugubriously out of the water and the mysterious, deep woods of the bottom lands beyond on the horizon. It seemed to me that I could see for miles. And the fact was, the lodge being built high upon wooden pilings, it was indeed possible to see great distances across the lake, which was five miles wide in places.

During those hours on the screened porch I would think about the tales I had heard the men tell the night before when they were gathered around the iron stove and when I was going off to sleep on my cot in a far corner of the room. I suppose the men must have been having their drinks then. But I can't say that I remember the smell of alcohol. All the smells there in that place were strange to me, though—the smell of the water outside, the smell of the whitewash on the vertical boarding on the lodge, and the smell of the musty rooms inside the lodge which stood empty most of the year. The tales the men told were often connected with the nightrider trouble. Others were old tales about the New Madrid Earthquake that had formed the Lake more than a hundred years before. Some of the men told old folk tales about prehistoric monsters that rose up out of the lake in the dark of the moon.

I don't recall my father's contributing to this talk. My memory is that he sat somewhat outside the circle, looking on and listening appreciatively to the talk of those older men, most of whom had probably never been outside the state of Tennessee, unless it was to go a little way up into Kentucky for whiskey. But my Grandfather Manley contributed his full share. And everyone listened to him with close attention. He spoke with an authority about the Lake, of course, that none of the others quite had. When those other men told their stories about prehistoric monsters rising from the lake, one felt almost that Grandfather when he emerged from his ten days in the swampland, according to his own account, must have looked and smelt like just such a prehistoric monster. To me the scariest of his talk was that about some of the hallucinations he had, hallucinations about the hooded men mounted on strange animals charging toward him like the horsemen of the apocalypse. But almost as frightening as his own reminiscences were the accounts he had heard or read of that earthquake that made the lake.

The earthquake had begun on December 16, 1811, and the sequence of shocks was felt as far away as Detroit and Baltimore and Charleston, South Carolina. Upriver, at New Madrid, Missouri, nearly the whole town crumbled down the bluffs and into the river. The shocks went on for many days—even for several months—and in between the shocks the earth vibrated and sometimes trembled for hours on end "like the flesh of a beef just killed." Men and women and children, during the first bad shocks, hung on to trees like squirrels. In one case a tree "infested with people" was seen to fall across a newly made ravine, and the poor wretches hung there for hours until there was a remission in the earth's undulation. Whole families were seen to disappear into round holes thirty feet wide, and the roaring of the upheaval was so loud that their screams could not be heard.

Between Memphis and St. Louis the river foamed and in some places the current was observed to have reversed and run upstream for several hours. Everywhere the quake was accompanied by a loud, hoarse roaring. And on land, where fissures and craters appeared, a black liquid was ejected sometimes to a height of fifteen feet and subsequently fell in a black shower, mixed with the sand which it had forced along with it. In other places the earth burst open, and mud, water, sandstone, and coal were thrown up the distance of thirty yards. Trees everywhere were blown up, cracking and splitting and falling by the thousands at a time. It was reported that in one place the black liquid oozed out of the ground to the height of the belly of a horse. Grandfather had heard or read somewhere that John James Audubon had been caught in some of the later, less violent shocks and that his horse died of fright with him sitting it. Numbers of people died, of course, on the river as well as on the land, and many of those who survived were never afterward regarded as possessing their right senses.

Among the hallucinations that my grandfather had while wandering in the low ground after his escape was that that earthquake of a hundred years before—almost to the day of the month—had recurred or commenced again, or that he was living in that earlier time when the whole earth seemed to be convulsed and its surface appeared as it must have in primordial times. And he imagined that he was there on that frontier in company with the ragged little bands of Frenchmen and Spaniards and newly arrived American settlers, all of whose settlements had vanished into the earth, all of them in flight, like so many Adams and Eves, before the wrath of their Maker.

My father told me more than one time—again, long after I was grown—that it was only after Grandfather Manley had had a few drinks and was off somewhere with a group of men that he would describe the times of wandering in the swamps and describe his hallucinations about the earthquake. And I myself heard him speak of those hallucinations, when I was at the lodge with them and was supposed to be asleep in my cot, heard him speak of them as though they were real events he had experienced and heard him say that his visions of the earthquake were like a glimpse into the eternal chaos we live in, a glimpse no man should be permitted, and that after that, all of his war experiences seemed small and insignificant matters—as nothing. And it was after that, of course, that he could never bring himself to go back to those reunions and take part in those reminiscences with the other old soldiers of events so much magnified by them each year or take part in their magnification of their own roles by advancing themselves in rank each year.

Grandfather could only confide those feelings of his to

other men. He would only confide them when he had a little whiskey in him. And what is important, too, is that he only drank alone or in the company of other men. He abhorred what my father and mother had come to speak of in the 1920s as social drinking. Drinking liquor was an evil and was a sign of weakness, he would have said, and just because one indulged in it oneself was no reason to pretend to the world that there was virtue in it. *That* to him was hypocrisy. Drinking behind closed doors or in a secluded hunting lodge, though one denounced it in public as an evil practice, signified respect for the public thing, which was more important than one's private character. It signified genuine humility.

And so it was, I must suppose, that he in some degree approved of the kind of drinking bout he had caught me in. And his approval, I suppose, spoiled the whole effect for me. It put me in the position, as I understand it now, of pretending to be like the man I felt myself altogether unlike and alien to.

And so it was that the circumstances he found me in were quite different on that inevitable Decoration Day visit of his. My parents were no sooner aboard the train for Memphis, that Friday night, than I had fetched a certain acquaintance of mine named Jeff Patterson—he was older than I and had finished his second year at Vanderbilt—and together we had picked up two girls we knew who lived on Eighth Avenue, near the Reservoir. We went dancing at a place out on Nine Mile Hill. We were joined there by two other couples of our acquaintance, and later the eight of us came back to Acklen Park. (I must say that I was much more experienced with girls by that age than I was with liquor.) We had had other, similar evenings at the house of the parents of the two other boys who joined us that night, but until then I had never been so bold as to use my parents' house for such purposes.

The girls we had with us were not the kind of girls such a boy as I was would spend any time with nowadays. That is why this part of the story may be difficult for people of a later generation to understand. With one's real girl, in those days, a girl who attended Ward Belmont school and who was enrolled in Miss Amy Lowe's dancing classes, one might neck in the back seat of a car. The girl might often respond too warmly and want to throw caution to the wind. But it was one's own manliness that made one overcome one's impulse to possess her and, most of all, overcome her impulse to let herself be possessed before taking the marriage vow. I am speaking of decent boys and girls of course and I acknowledge that even among decent or "nice" young people of that day there were exceptions to the rule. One knew of too many seven-month babies to have any doubt of that. Still, from the time one was fourteen or fifteen in Nashville, one had to know girls of various sorts and one had to have a place to take girls of the "other sort." No one of my generation would have been shocked by the events of that evening. The four couples went to bed—and finally slept—in the four bedrooms on the second floor of my parents' house in Acklen Park. As I have indicated, I had never before brought such a party to our house, and I gave no thought to how I would clean up the place afterward or how I would conceal what had gone on there.

It was only a few minutes past seven the next morning when I heard Grandfather's car outside in the driveway. I was at once electrified and paralyzed by the sound. Lying there in my own bed with that girl beside me, and with the other couples still asleep in the other rooms, I had a vision of our big, two-story brick house as it appeared from the outside that May morning, saw the details of the stone coigns at the four corners of the house, the heavy green window blinds and the keystones above the windows, even the acanthus leaves in the capitals of the columns on the front porch. I saw it all through my grandfather's sharp little eyes as he turned into the gravel driveway, and saw through his eyes not only my parents' car, which I had carelessly left out of the garage, but the cars also of the two other boys who had joined us, all three cars sitting out there in the driveway on Sunday morning, as if to announce to him that some kind of party—and even *what* kind of party, probably—was going on inside.

He didn't step into his room to set down his Gladstone bag. I heard him drop it on the floor in the front hall and then I heard his quick footstep on the long stairway. Then I heard him opening the doors to all the bedrooms. (We *had* had the decency to close ourselves off in separate rooms.) He opened my door last, by design I suppose. I was lying on my stomach and I didn't even lift my head to look at him. But I knew exactly how he would appear there in the doorway, still wearing his long coat and his summer straw hat. That was the last thought or the last vision I indulged in before I felt the first blow of his walking stick across my buttocks. At last he had struck me! That was what I thought to myself. At last we might begin to understand one another and make known our real feelings, each about the other.

By the time I felt the second blow from his stick I had realized that between the two blows he delivered me he had struck one on the buttocks of the girl beside me. Already I had begun to understand that his striking me didn't have quite the kind of significance I had imagined. By the time he had struck the girl a second time she had begun screaming. I came up on my elbows and managed to clamp my hand over her mouth to keep the neighbors from hearing her. He left us then. And over his shoulder as he went striding from the room he said, "I want you to get these bitches out of this house and to do so in one hell of a hurry!" He went back into the hallway, and then when I had scrambled out of bed I saw him, to my baffling chagrin and unaccountable sense of humiliation, hurrying into the other rooms, first one and then another, and delivering blows to the occupants of those other beds. Some of the others, I suppose, had heard him crack the door to their rooms earlier and had crawled out of bed before he got there. But I heard him and saw him wielding his stick against Jeff Patterson's backsides and against the little bottom of the girl beside him. Finally—still wearing his hat and his gabardine coat, mind you—he passed through the hall again and toward the head of the stair. I was standing in the doorway to my room by then, but still clad only in my underwear shorts. As he went down the stairsteps he glanced back at me and spoke again: "You get those bitches out of your mother's house and you do it in one hell of a hurry."

Even before I was able to pull on my clothes, all four of the girls were fully dressed and scurrying down the stairs, followed immediately by the three boys. I came to the head of the stairs and stood there somewhat bemused, looking down. The girls had gone off into the front rooms downstairs in search of certain of their possessions. I heard them calling to each other desperately, "I left my lipstick right here on this table!" And, "Oh, God, where's my purse?" And, "Where in the world are my pumps?" I realized then that one of them had gone down the stairs barefoot, and simultaneously I saw Grandfather Manley moving by the foot of the stairs and toward the living room.

I descended slowly, listening to the voices in the front room. First there had come a little shriek from one of the girls when Grandfather entered. Then I heard his voice reassuring them. By the time I reached the living-room doorway he was assisting them in their search, whereas the three boys only stood by, watching. It was he himself who found that little purse. Already the four girls seemed completely at ease. He spoke to them gently and without contempt or even condescension. The girl who had been my date left with the others, without either of us raising the question of whether or not I might see her home. As they went out through the wide front door the four girls called out, "Goodbye!" in cheerful little voices. I opened my mouth to respond, but before I could make a sound I heard Grandfather answering, "Goodbye, girls." And it came over me that it had been to him, not me, they were calling goodbye. When he and I were alone in the hall, he said, "And now I reckon you realize what we've got to do. We've got to do something about those sheets."

It is a fact that he and I spent a good part of that day doing certain clean-up jobs and employing the electric iron here and there. I can't say it drew us together, though, or made any sort of bond between us. Perhaps that's what he imagined the result would be. But I never imagined so for a moment. I knew that one day there was something he would have to know about me that he couldn't forgive. Though he and I were of the same blood, we had parted company, so to speak, before I was born even, and there was some divisive thing between us that could never be overcome. Perhaps I felt that day that it was my parents, somehow, who would forever be a wall between us, and that once any people turned away from what he was, as they had done, then that—whatever it was he was—was lost to them and to their children and their children's children forever. But I cannot say definitely that I felt anything so certain or grand that day. I cannot say for sure what I felt except that when he spoke with such composure and assurance to those girls in my parents' living room, I felt that there was nothing in the world he didn't know and hadn't been through.

As he and I worked away at cleaning up the bedrooms

that morning, I asked myself if his knowing so well how to speak to those girls and if the genuine sympathy and even tenderness that he clearly felt toward them meant perhaps that his insistence upon living alone in that old house over in Hunt County suggested there were girls or women in his life still. Whatever else his behavior that day meant, it meant that the more bad things I did and the worse they were, then the better he would think he understood me and the more alike he would think we were. But I knew there was yet something I could do that would show him how different we were and that until I had made him grasp that, I would not begin to discover what, since I wasn't and couldn't be like him, I *was* like. Or if, merely as a result of being born when I was and where I was, at the very tail end of something, I was like nothing else at all, only incomparably without a character of my own.

In July, Mother and Father went up to Beersheba Springs, on the Cumberland Plateau, for a few days' relief from the hot weather. Beersheba was an old-fashioned watering place, the resort in past times of Episcopal bishops, Louisiana planters, and the gentry of Middle Tennessee. By the 1920s only a select few from the Nashville Basin kept cottages there and held sway at the old hotel. It was the kind of summer spot my parents felt most comfortable in. It had never had the dash of Tate Springs or the homey atmosphere of Monteagle, but it was older than either of those places and had had since its beginning gambling tables, horses, and dancing. Behind the porticoed hotel on the bluff's edge the old slave quarters were still standing, as was also the two-story brick garconnière, reached by a covered walkway from the hotel. There was an old graveyard overgrown with box and red cedar, enclosed by a rock wall and containing old gravestones leaning at precarious angles but still bearing good Tennessee-

Virginia names like Burwell and Armistead. Farther along
the bluff and farther back on the plateau were substantial
cottages and summer houses, a good number of them built
of squared chestnut logs and flanked by handsome limestone end-chimneys. The ancient and unreconstructed
atmosphere of the place had its attraction even for Grandfather Manley, and my parents had persuaded him to ac-
company them on their holiday there.

He drove in to Nashville and then, still in his own car,
followed Mother and Father in their car to Beersheba
Springs, which was seventy or eighty miles southeast of
Nashville, on the edge of the Plateau and just above what
used to be known as the Highland Rim. It seemed a long
way away. There was no question in my mind of the old
man's turning up in Nashville this time. I looked forward
with pleasure to a few days of absolute freedom—from my
parents, from my grandfather, and even from the servants,
who were always given a holiday whenever my parents
were out of town. I was in such relaxed good spirits when
Father and Mother and Grandfather Manley had departed
that I went up to my room—though it was not yet noon—
and took a nap on my bed. I had no plans made for this
period of freedom except to see even more than usual of a
Ward Belmont girl with whom I had been having dates
during most of that winter and spring and whom my parents, as an indication of their approval of my courting a
girl of her particular family, had had to dinner at our house
several times and even on one occasion when my grandfather was there. She was acknowledged by my family and
by everyone else to be my girl, and by no one more ex-
pressly than by the two of us—by the girl herself, that is,
and by myself.

I was awakened from my nap just before noon that day
by the ringing of the telephone in the upstairs hall. And it
so happened that the person calling was none other than

she whom I would have most wished to hear from. It was not usual for such a girl to telephone any boy, not even her acknowledged favorite. I have to say that as soon as I heard her voice I experienced one of those moments I used often to have in my youth, of seeming to know how everything was going to go. I can't blame myself for how things did go during the next twenty-four hours and can't blame the girl, either. Since this is not the story of our romance, it will suffice to say that though our romance did not endure for long after that time, these events were not necessarily the cause for its failure. The girl herself has prospered in life quite as much as I have. And no doubt she sometimes speaks of me nowadays, wherever in the world she is living, as "a boy I went with in Nashville," without ever actually mentioning my name. At any rate, when she telephoned that day she said she was *very much* upset about something and wanted *very much* to see me at once. She apologized for calling. She would not have been so brash, she said, except that since I had told her of my parents' plans she knew I would probably be at home alone. The circumstance about which she was upset was that since her parents, too, were out of town, her two older sisters were planning "an awful kind of party" that she could not possibly have any part in. She wanted me to help her decide what she must do.

My parents had taken our family car to Beersheba, and so it was that she and I had to meet on foot, halfway between Acklen Park and her home, which was two or three miles away, out in the Belle Meade section. And it ended, of course, after several hours of earnest talk about love and life—exchanged over milkshakes in a place called Candy Land and on the benches in the Japanese Garden in Centennial Park—ended, that is, by our coming to my house and telephoning her sisters that she had gone to spend the night with a classmate from Ward Belmont. The inevitability of its working out so is beyond question in my mind. At least, in retrospect it is. Certainly both of us had known for many days beforehand that both sets of parents would be out of town; and certainly the very passionate kind of necking which we had been indulging in that summer, in the darkness of my father's car and in the darkness of her father's back terrace, had become almost intolerable to us. But we could honestly say to ourselves that we had made no plans for that weekend. We were able to tell ourselves afterward that it was just something that happened. And I was able to tell myself for many years afterward—I cannot deny it categorically even today—that I would not have consented to our coming to my house if I had thought there were the remotest possibility of Grandfather Manley's turning up there.

And yet, though I can tell myself so, there will always be a certain lingering doubt in my mind. And even after it was clear to both of us that we would sleep together that night, her sense of propriety was still such that she refused to go up to the second floor of my house. Even when I led her into Grandfather Manley's room, she did not realize or did not acknowledge to herself that it was a bedroom we were in. I suppose she had never before seen anything quite like the furniture there. "What a darling room!" she exclaimed when I had put on the floor lamp beside the golden-oak rocker. And when I pulled down the great folding bed, even in the dim lamplight I could see that she blushed. Simultaneously almost, I caught a glimpse of myself in the mirror of the oak bureau and I cannot deny that I thought with certain glee in that moment of my grandfather or deny that I felt a certain premonition of events.

My first thought when I heard his car outside the next afternoon was, We are in *his* room! We are in *his* bed! I imagined that that was what was going to disturb him most. The fact was we had been in and out of his bed I don't know how many times by then. We had not only made love there in a literal sense, and were so engaged when he arrived, but we had during various intervals delighted each other there in the bed with card games and even checkers and Parcheesi, with enormous quantities of snacks which the cook had left for me in the refrigerator, and finally with reading aloud to each other from volumes of poetry and fiction which I fetched from my room upstairs. If there had been any sense of wrongdoing in our heads the previous afternoon, regarding such preoccupations as would be ours during those two days, it had long since been dispelled by the time that old man my grandfather arrived—dispelled for both of us, and not just for that time but probably for all future time. (As for myself, I know that I never again in all the years since have had any taste for taking my pleasure with such females as those Eighth Avenue– Reservoir girls—in the casual, impersonal way that one does with such females of any class or age.)

When I told her there beside me that it was the tires of my grandfather's car she and I had heard skidding in the gravel and that it was now his quick, light step on the porch steps that I recognized, she seized me by the wrist and whispered, "Even if he knows I'm here, I don't want him to see me, and I don't want to see him. You have to hide me! Quickly!" By the time we had pushed up the folding bed, there was already the sound of his key in the front door. There was nothing for it, if she were to be hidden, but to hide her in the wardrobe.

"Over there," I said, "if you're sure you want to. But it's his room. He's apt to find you."

"Don't you let him," she commanded.

"You put on your clothes," was all I could say. I was pulling on my trousers. And now she was running on tip-toe toward the wardrobe, with nothing on at all, carrying all her clothing and a pillow and blanket from the bed, all in a bundle clutched before her. She opened the wardrobe door, tossed. everything in before her, and then hopped in on top of it. I followed her over there, buttoning my trousers and trying to get into my shirt. As I took a last step forward to close the door on her, I realized that, except for her and the bundle of clothing she was crouched on, the wardrobe was entirely empty. There were no possessions of Grandfather's in it. I thought to myself, Perhaps he never opens the wardrobe, even. And as I closed the door I saw to my delight that my brave girl, huddled there inside the wardrobe, wasn't by any means shedding tears but was smiling up at me. And I think I knew then for the first time in my life how wonderful it is to be in love and how little anything else in the world matters. And I found myself smiling back at her with hardly an awareness of the fact that she hadn't a piece of clothing on her body. And I actually delayed closing the door long enough to put the palm of my hand to my mouth and throw her a kiss.

Then, having observed the emptiness of the wardrobe, I glanced over at the oak bureau and wondered if it weren't entirely empty, too. I was inspired by that thought to quickly gather up my books, along with a bread wrapper and a jam jar, a kitchen knife, a couple of plates and glasses, and also my own shoes and socks, and to stuff them all inside a drawer of the bureau. On opening the heavy top drawer I found I was not mistaken. The drawer was empty and with no sign of its ever having been used by Grandfather—perhaps not since the day when the furniture had first been brought from Hunt County and Mother had put down the white paper in it for lining.

Already I had heard Grandfather Manley calling my name out in the front hall. It was something I think he had never done before when arriving at the house. His choosing to do so had given me the extra time I had needed. When I closed the big bureau drawer I looked at myself in the wide mirror above it, and I was almost unrecognizable even to myself. I was sweating profusely. My hair was uncombed. I had not shaved in two days. My trousers and shirt were all wrinkles. But I heard my grandfather calling me a second time and knew I had to go out there.

When I stepped, barefoot, into his view I could tell from his expression that he saw me just as I had seen myself and that I was barely recognizable to him. He was standing at the foot of the stairs, from which point he had been calling my name. No doubt my face showed him how astonished I was to have him call out to me on coming into the house—at the informality and open friendliness of it. No doubt for a minute or so he supposed that accounted wholly for my obvious consternation. He actually smiled at me. It was rather a sickly grin, though, like General Forrest's, the smile of a man who isn't given to smiling. And yet there was an undeniable warmth in his smile and in the total expression on his face. "I couldn't abide another day of Beersheba Springs," he said. "The swells over there are too rich for my blood. I thought I would just slip by here on my way home and see what kind of mischief you might be up to."

Clearly what he said was intended to amuse me. And just as clearly he meant that he preferred whatever low life he might find me engaged in to the high life led by my parents' friends at Beersheba. Presently, though, he could deceive himself no longer about my extraordinary appearance and my nervous manner's indication that something was wrong.

"What's the matter, son?" he said.

"Nothing's the matter," I said belligerently.

The very friendliness of his demeanor somehow made me resent more bitterly than ever before his turning up at so inconvenient a moment. This was my real life he had come in on and was interfering with. Moreover, he had

intruded this time with real and unconcealed feelings of
his own. I could not permit him, at that hour of my life,
to make me the object of his paternal affection. I was a
grown man now and was in love with a girl who was about
to be disgraced in his eyes. How could there be anything
between him and me? His life, whether or not it was in
any way his fault, had kept him from knowing what love
of our sort was. He might know everything else in the
world, including every other noble feeling which I could
never be able to experience. He might be morally correct
about everything else in the world, but he was not morally
correct about love between a man and a woman. This was
what I felt there in the hall that afternoon. I was aware of
how little I had to base my judgment on. It was based
mostly on the nothing that had ever been said about women
in all the stories he had told me. In all the stories about
the nightriders, for instance, there was no incident about
his reunion with his wife, my grandmother, afterward. And
I never heard him speak of her by her first name. Even
now I wonder how we ever know about such men and
their attitude toward women. In our part of the world we
were all brought up on tales of the mysterious ways of
Thomas Jefferson, whose mother and wife are scarcely
mentioned in his writings, and Andrew Jackson and Sam
Houston, whose reticence on the subject of women is beyond the comprehension of most men nowadays. Did they
have too much respect for women? Were they perhaps, for
all their courage in other domains, afraid of women or
afraid of their own compelling feelings about women? I
didn't think all of this, of course, as I faced Grandfather
Manley there in the hall, but I believe I felt it. It seemed
to me that his generation and my own were a thousand
years apart.

"What's the matter, son?" he said.

"Nothing's the matter," I said.

There was nothing more for either of us to say. He began to move toward me and in the direction of his room. "Why don't you wait a minute," I said, "before you go into your room?"

His little eyes widened, and after a moment he said, "It ain't my room, y' know. I only stay in it."

"Yes," I said, "but I've been reading in there. Let me go clear up my books and things." I had no idea but to delay him. I said, "Maybe you should go out to the kitchen and get something to eat."

But he walked right past me, still wearing his hat and coat, of course, and still carrying his little Gladstone bag. When he had passed into his room and I had followed him in there, he said, "I see no books and things."

"No," I said, "I hid them in the bureau drawer. I didn't know whether you would like my being in here."

He looked at me skeptically. I went over and opened the drawer and took out my books and my shoes and socks. Then I closed the drawer, leaving everything else in it. But he came and opened the drawer again. And he saw the plates and other things. "What else are you hiding?" he asked. No doubt he had heard the knives and the plates rattling about when I closed the drawer. Then he turned and walked over to the wardrobe. I ran ahead of him and placed myself against the door. "You've got one of those bitches of yours hidden in there, I reckon," he said.

"No, sir," I said, trying to look him straight in the eye.

"Then what is it?" he said. And he began blinking his eyes, not because I was staring into them but because he was thinking, "Are you going to tell me, or am I going to find out for myself?"

Suddenly I said, "It's my girl in there." We were both silent for a time, staring into each other's eyes. "And you've no right to open the door on her," I finally said. "Because she's not dressed."

"You're lying," he came back at me immediately. "I don't believe you for a minute." He left me and went to the folding bed and pulled it down. He set his bag on the bed and he poked at the jumble of sheets with his cane. Then he stood there, looking back at me for several moments. He still had not removed his straw hat and had not unbuttoned his coat. Finally he began moving across the room toward me. He stood right before me, looking me in the eye again. Then, with almost no effort, he pushed me aside and opened the wardrobe door.

She still hadn't managed to get into her clothes but she was hugging the pillow and had the blanket half pulled over her shoulder. I think he may have recognized her from the one time he had met her at dinner. Or maybe, I thought to myself, he was just such an old expert that he could tell what kind of girl she was from one glance at her. Anyway, he turned on me a look cold and fierce and so articulate that I imagined I could hear the words his look expressed: "So this is how bad you really are?" Then he went directly over to the bed, took up his bag and his cane, left the room, and left the house without speaking to me again.

When I had heard the front door close I took the leather ottoman across the room and sat on it, holding hands with that brave and quiet girl who, with the door wide open now, remained crouching inside the wardrobe. When finally we heard him drive out of the driveway we smiled at each other and kissed. And I thought to myself again that his generation and ours were a thousand years apart, or ten thousand.

I THOUGHT OF COURSE THAT WHEN GRAND-father Manley left Acklen Park he would continue on his way to Hunt County. But that was not the case. Or probably he did go to Hunt County, after all, and then turned around and went back to Beersheba Springs from there.

Because he arrived at Beersheba at about eleven o'clock
that night, and it would be difficult to explain how he was
dressed as he was unless he had made a trip home and
changed into the clothes he arrived in. He left Acklen Park
about four in the afternoon, and from that time through
the remaining ten years of his life he was never again seen
wearing the old gabardine coat or either of his broad-
brimmed hats. When he arrived at Beersheba, Mother and
Father were sitting on the front gallery of the hotel with
a group of friends. They were no doubt rocking away in
the big rockers that furnished the porch, talking about the
bridge hands they had held that evening, and enjoying the
view of the moonlit valley below Cumberland Mountain.

When they saw him drive up, the car was unmistakable
of course. But the man who emerged from it was not unmistakable. Major Basil Manley was dressed in a black
serge suit, and in the starched collar of his white shirt he
wore a black shoestring tie. I can describe his attire in such
detail because from that day I never saw him in any other.
That is, except on Decoration Day in those later years,
when he invariably appeared in Confederate uniform. And
in which uniform, at his own request, he was finally buried,
not at Huntsboro and not in the family graveyard, but at
Mount Olivet Cemetery, at Nashville. My father's account
of his arrival on the hotel porch is memorable to me because it is the source of a great discovery which I felt I had
made. My parents didn't recognize him for a certainty until
he had passed along the shadowy brick walkway between
the hovering boxwoods and stepped up on the porch. And
then, significantly, both of them went to him and kissed
him on the cheek, first my mother and then my father.
And all the while, as my father described it, Major Manley
stood there, ramrod straight, his cheeks wet with tears, like
an old general accepting total defeat with total fortitude.

And what I understood for certain when I heard about

that ceremony of theirs was that it had, after all, been their battle all along, his and theirs, not his and mine. I, after all, had only been the pawn of that gentle-seeming couple who were his daughter and son-in-law and who were my parents. It is almost unbelievable the changes that took place in Grandfather from that day. He grew his beard again, which was completely white now, of course. It hid his lean jaw and weak chin, making him very handsome, and was itself very beautiful in its silky whiteness against his black suit and black shoestring tie. The following year— the very next May—he began attending the Confederate Reunions again. And of course he was promptly promoted to the rank of colonel. Yet he did hold out against ever wearing the insignia of that rank, until he was in his coffin and it was put on him by other hands. So far as I know he never allowed anyone—not even the other veterans—to address him other than as Major Manley. And in the fall after he had first appeared in his new role at Beersheba Springs, he began coming in to Nashville more often than ever. I was not at home that fall, since that was my first year away at college, but when I would go home for a weekend and find him there or find that he had been there, I would observe some new object in his room, an old picture of my grandmother as a girl, bare-shouldered and with dark curls about her face, the picture in its original oval frame. Other family pictures soon appeared, too. And there was a handsome washbasin and pitcher, and there were some of his favorite books, like Ramsay's *Annals of Tennessee* and lawbooks that had belonged to his father, my great-grandfather. And then, very soon, he began to bring in small pieces of furniture that were unlike the golden-oak pieces already there.

When my mother had first urged Grandfather Manley to come live with us, it was just after my grandmother died and before we had moved into the big house in Acklen

Park. He had said frankly then that he thought he would find it too cramped in our little house on Division Street. But when they bought the new house, they had done so with an eye to providing accommodations that would be agreeable to an old man who might before many years not like to climb stairs and who, at any rate, was known to be fond of his privacy. They consulted with a number of their friends who had the responsibility for aging parents. It was a bond they were now going to share with those friends or a bond which they aspired to, anyway. In those days in Nashville, having a Confederate veteran around the place was comparable to having a peacock on the lawn or, if not that, at least comparable to having one's children in the right schools. It was something anybody liked to have. It didn't matter, I suppose, what rank the veteran was, since he was certain to be promoted as the years passed. The pressure on Major Manley to move in with his daughter and son-in-law was gentle always, but it was constant and it was enduring. One of the most compelling reasons given him was they wanted him to get to know his only grandson and that they wanted the grandson to have the benefit of growing up in the house with him. Well, when the new house was bought and he was shown that room on the first floor which was to be reserved perpetually for him whenever he might choose to come and occupy it, and when he was urged to furnish it with whatever pieces he might wish to bring in from Hunt County, he no doubt felt he could not absolutely reject the invitation. And he no doubt had unrealistic dreams about some kind of rapport that might develop between him and the son of this daughter and son-in-law of his. I don't remember the day it happened of course, but it must have come as a considerable shock and disappointment to Mother when a truck hired in Huntsboro arrived, bearing not the rosewood half-canopied bed from her mother's room at home, or the cannonball four-poster from the guest room there, but the fold-away golden-oak piece that came instead, and the other golden-oak pieces that arrived instead of the walnut and mahogany pieces she had had in mind. Yet no complaint was made to the old man. (His daughter and son-in-law were much too gentle for that.) The golden oak had come out of the downstairs "office" in the old farmhouse, which he had furnished when he first got married and moved in with his own parents. No doubt he thought it most appropriate for any downstairs bedroom, even in Acklen Park. The main object was to get him to occupy the room. And, after his fashion, this of course was how he had occupied it through the years.

But by Christmas of the year he and I had our confrontations he had, piece by piece, moved all new furnishings into the room and had disposed of all the golden oak. The last piece he exchanged was the folding bed for the walnut cannonball bed. When I came home at Christmas, there was the big four-poster filling the room, its mattress so high above the floor (in order to accommodate the trundle bed) that a set of walnut bed steps was required for Grandfather to climb into or out of it. And before spring came the next year Grandfather had closed his house in Hunt County and taken up permanent residence in Acklen Park. He lived there for the rest of his life, participating in my parents' lively social activities, talking freely about his Civil War experiences, even telling the ladies how he courted my grandmother during that time, and how sometimes he would slip away from his encampment, make a dash for her father's farm, and spy on her from the edge of a wood without ever letting her know he had been in the neighborhood.

Such anecdotes delighted the Nashville ladies and the Nashville gentlemen, too. But often he would talk seriously and at length about the War itself—to the great and special delectation of both my parents—describing for a room full of people the kind of lightning warfare that Forrest carried on, going on late into the evening sometimes, describing every little crossroads skirmish from Between The Rivers to Shiloh, pausing now and then for a little parenthetical explanation, for the ladies, of such matters as the difference between tactics and strategy. Sometimes he would display remarkable knowledge of the grand strategy of the really great battles of the War, of Shiloh and Vicksburg, of Stone River, Franklin, and Chickamauga, and of other battles that he had no part in. When he had a sufficiently worthy audience he would even speculate about whether or not the War in the West might have been won if Bragg had been removed from his command or whether the whole War mightn't have been won if President Davis had not viewed it so narrowly from the Richmond point of view. Or he would raise the question of what might have happened if Lee had been allowed to go to the Mountains.

I heard my parents' accounts of all such talk of his. But I heard some of it myself, too. The fall after I had graduated from Wallace School, I went away to the University of the South, at Sewanee. My father had gone to Vanderbilt because he had been a Methodist, and Vanderbilt was the great Methodist university in those days. But he and Mother, under the influence of one of his aunts, had become Episcopalian before I was born even. And so there was never any idea but that I should go to Sewanee. I liked being at Sewanee and liked being away from Nashville for the first time in my life. The University of course was full of boys from the various states of the Deep South. I very soon made friends there with boys from Mississippi and Louisiana and South Carolina. And since Nashville was so close by, I used to bring some of them home with me on weekends or on short holidays. They of course had never seen Grandfather Manley the way he had been before. And they couldn't imagine his being different from the way he was then. He would gather us around him sometimes in the evening and talk to us about the War Between the States. The boys loved to listen to him. They really adored him and made over him and clamored for him to tell certain stories over and over again. I enjoyed it, too, of course. He seemed quite as strange and interesting an old character to me as he did to them. And sometimes when I would ask him a question, just the way the others did, he would answer me with the same politeness he showed them, and at those times I would have the uneasy feeling that he wasn't quite certain whether it was I or one of the others who was his grandson, whether I was not perhaps merely one of the boys visiting, with the others, from Sewanee.

ABOUT THE AUTHOR

Peter Taylor was born in Tennessee in 1917. He is the author of seven books of stories, including THE COLLECTED STORIES OF PETER TAYLOR, A LONG FOURTH, MISS LEONORA WHEN LAST SEEN, IN THE MIRO DISTRICT and THE OLD FOREST AND OTHER STORIES; the novels A WOMAN OF MEANS and A SUMMONS TO MEMPHIS; and four books of plays. Mr. Taylor has taught at Harvard University, at the University of North Carolina, and at Kenyon College, from which he was graduated in 1940. Since 1967, he has been Commonwealth Professor of English at the University of Virginia; he spends his winters in Key West. In 1985, the National Endowment for the Arts honored him as a ''senior fellow.'' He lives with his wife, the poet Eleanor Ross Taylor, in Charlottesville, Virginia.

The Undisputed Masters of Contemporary Fiction